PUBLISHING

A Dash OF Love

Liz Isaacson

Based on the Hallmark Channel Original Movie
Teleplay by Sandra Berg & Judith Berg
Story by Sib Ventress

ISBN: 978-1-947892-06-4

www.hallmarkpublishing.com
For more about the movie visit:
www.hallmarkchannel.com/a-dash-of-love

Chapter One

Nikki Turner moved around the small kitchen in the diner with ease, the space familiar and cozy. She glanced up as the bell rang again, wondering where in the world Gus was going to put all these customers. She noticed a family bustling by the diner in their winter gear, and she mourned the fact that she'd be working long past the time when the sun would set. Shame, too, when it was shining so brightly, a welcome sight after the gloomy winter they'd been having in Lakeside.

The scent of spaghetti drew her gaze from the front windows, reminding her that the orders were still piled up.

Nikki enjoyed her time in the diner, making sandwiches, slinging pie for the couples celebrating Valentine's Day a few weeks early, and ladling chili into bowls. In fact, she couldn't think of anything else she'd rather be doing.

Every seat in Gus's Kitchen had been occupied for hours, and that bell kept ringing like there was room for more. Nikki smiled as a couple who'd come in to Gus's every week for the past year greeted the restaurant's namesake and started speaking with him.

A rush of affection for the white-haired man slowed Nikki down for about two seconds. Then she put together the Kitchen's signature sandwich: pastrami and turkey with tomatoes, olives, and a special spread she'd developed over the course of six months and a lot of feedback from Gus's regulars. She grinned at the sandwich like they were old friends before setting it in the window for pickup.

She garnished her signature, secret-recipe chili with a healthy dollop of sour cream and a generous sprinkling of chopped scallions. She wanted to sneak a tortilla chip, but just because she hadn't been to culinary school didn't mean she didn't take herself seriously as a cook. She'd been working in a commercial kitchen for years, and a pro would never snack while on the job.

She put up the bowl of chili as a rousing cheer for Gus rose into the rafters. A thread of sadness pulled through her as she thought about going home tonight and not coming back to this diner where she'd worked for a year and a half. She kept the smile on her face, though, as she grabbed the next ticket from the old-school holder.

Nikki managed to chase away her worries by working as quickly as she could, getting the food out to the customers without delay, and trading quips with Angela. The waitress had become Nikki's best friend when Nikki had started at Gus's eighteen months ago, and they'd moved in together very soon after that. Angela was fun, sarcastic, and the perfect roommate for Nikki and all her quirks. And soon, they'd both be out of a job.

At least Angela had already found something else to pay the bills. Nikki, however, was having a much harder time getting something that aligned her career goals, her passion for food, and her absent degree.

Someone waved for her to come out of the kitchen, and she went to congratulate Gus while the crowd was still thick. Angela hugged him in front of the huge, multicolored *Farewell Gus!* banner, and then Nikki embraced him. He reminded her so much of her own grandfather, from the wispy white hair right down to the smell of clean and crisp dryer sheets. She wished this restaurant wasn't closing—wished she'd been able to bring it to a different ending.

But she refused to let any of her sadness show and stepped back into the kitchen. She felt most at home here, and her melancholy lifted like the steam off the huge pot of chili to her right.

By the time the restaurant closed, Nikki's pinky toe pinched in her shoes, and her back ached for a healthy dose of ibuprofen. Angela stood at the bar, putting glasses into a bin, and Nikki exhaled heavily as she sat across from her best friend.

"Has to have been our busiest day ever." She put her coat on the stool next to her and glanced over to a busboy saying his final goodbye to Gus.

Angela leaned on the counter. "It certainly was our best tip day ever!" She tossed a napkin into the bin beside her.

"Well, get used to it, Ang. You're gonna be making a lot of tips at a place like Holly Hanson's." Though exhaustion nearly consumed her, the smile wouldn't leave Nikki's face. So this chapter was closing. She felt certain a new one would open for her the same way Ang had found a job at Holly Hanson's, the premier restaurant in the city.

Nikki had entertained the idea of applying at Holly Hanson's for about point-four seconds. But they had real chefs with tall white hats and pieces of paper testifying to their skill with a knife, spices, and flavor combinations.

"It's definitely a perk," Angela said. "But I am going to miss working with you, though."

"And I'm going to miss working." Nikki tucked her reddish-brown hair behind her ear. "I didn't get the job at Café Rouge."

Angela was kind enough to look shocked. She even sounded it when she said, "I thought they really liked you."

Nikki's smile faded. "They did, but they just don't like that I don't have a culinary degree." No one liked that, it seemed.

"That is so unfair." Her light eyes flashed with indignation. "You are, hands down, the best cook I know. And I've worked at a lot of restaurants."

Nikki shrugged and tried not to focus on the negative. She glanced around the restaurant that had become her refuge, grateful for the time she'd had here. "I sure am going to miss this place. They just don't make diners like this anymore."

Gus sidled over as Angela took her bin of dishes and trash into the kitchen, the rest of the employees finally slipping away into the night. "Not too late to take it on. I'm telling ya, someone is gonna come in and turn the place into a juice bar or something." He looked horrified at the thought, as if juice were the wrong liquid to consume at all, ever.

Sympathy settled in Nikki's heart. "Oh, Gus. You know I wish I could." And she'd never meant anything more sincerely. But working as a cook and making her own way in the city didn't leave her much money to buy a restaurant. "It certainly is a dream of mine to own a place like this one day." She watched as a waitress took the bunch of balloons floating outside the diner and walked away from Gus's. "But I don't have the money. Not to mention the lack of business experience."

"Business can be learned," Gus said in his wise voice. "But talent? That's something that just comes as a gift to you. And you, kiddo—you are talented. So you just keep your eye on the prize, and someday I'm sure you'll get your dream."

Nikki's smile returned in full force. She'd been lucky to know Gus, and she hoped she'd see him around the city after today. In fact, she made a mental note to make sure she did.

"Just don't forget to let me know when that happens." Gus leaned forward, his face open and kind. "I may be retiring, but I'll never be too old to come and have some of your chili." He covered both of her hands with one of his. Nikki's heartstrings squeezed, and she masked her tears behind an affectionate smile.

"Speaking of chili," he said. "Will you finally tell me what your secret ingredient is?"

Nikki gave a little chuckle and tilted her head to the side. "Cinnamon candy."

"The ones I keep by the cash register for the customers?"

"Those are the ones," Nikki singsonged.

Gus chuckled and shook his head. "Well, that would explain why the jar was always empty."

As they laughed together, he switched off the last of the lights in the diner.

Nikki admired the framed menu of Gus's Kitchen she'd just picked up from the custom art shop down the street. She hung it next to the menu from King of the Court and above Alfredo & Sons.

Gus's made five framed menus, and Nikki took a

moment to think about her time at each restaurant. She possessed experience in spades. Surely, someone would see that. Soon.

Sunlight streamed through the front windows of the apartment, declaring another day had begun. Another day without a job. Another day closer to Valentine's Day. She banished the thoughts of her least favorite holiday before they could infringe on her good mood.

Angela came out of her bedroom and stalled at the sight of the bright red toaster on the table. She eyed it for a moment and then sat down. "Another toaster? Where'd you get this one?"

Nikki admired it. "Got it at the flea market yesterday. Beautiful, isn't it?" She really didn't have a lot of money to be spending on frivolous things like toasters, but she did have a lot of time on her hands. And if wandering through Lakeside and looking at antiques made her happy, why shouldn't she do it?

Angela poured herself a cup of coffee and returned to the table. "So, what's wrong with modern toasters?" She took a sip and glanced at Nikki like she already knew the answer.

Nikki shrugged, her voice much too high when she said, "Nothing. The older ones just brown more evenly."

Angela only barely refrained from rolling her eyes. "Right. You do know that our place is starting to look like a diner museum, don't you?" Her playful tone told

Nikki that she didn't really care that it appeared as if a fifties diner had thrown up in their apartment.

"I'm sorry," Nikki said, a plea in her voice. "It's that I see all these things, and I just can't help but picture them in my own restaurant one day. I can't help myself." She nudged the frame a bit to the right and cocked her head to see if the menu was straight. She pushed it left again and backed away from it.

But now some of the others looked crooked. "So how was work yesterday?" She made minute adjustments to each frame.

Angela exhaled. "Tense. Going from Gus's Kitchen to Holly Hanson's is definitely a challenge. Last night, she yelled at me for carrying too many plates on my arm." She spoke with an incredulous note in her voice and took another sip from her mug.

Nikki thought for a moment. "Well, Holly Hanson's is formal dining, so I kinda see her point." Not that she'd ever been a waitress. Or eaten often in such a ritzy setting. Maybe she shouldn't have said anything.

Angela gave her a look that said she was going to let that comment pass because of their friendship. "Listen, hate to break it to you, but your favorite chef isn't the nicest chef in town." She tossed her dark brown hair over her shoulder.

Nikki abandoned the fruitless quest to ensure all the menus hung in perfectly straight lines. Disbelief tore through her. "Really?"

Angela looked a bit pained. "Really." She sighed in an I-can't-believe-I-have-to-go-back-there-tonight kind of way. "She's condescending, and she's got this diva quality about her. And to tell you the truth, you're a better chef than her."

"No, I'm a cook, not a chef." Nikki shook her head and picked up her favorite coffee mug, a tall green piece of stoneware with hand-painted red and purple flowers on it.

"Tomato, tomahto. Point is, her recipes aren't even that great."

Nikki was halfway to lifting her mug to her lips when she paused. Shock traveled through her. "Okay, I don't believe that."

She ignored Angela's little half-shrug and kept going. "I mean, she just, she came out of nowhere, and she built an entire brand. She's an award-winning chef. She's opened up an entire restaurant, and—and she's published four cookbooks in four years. It's amazing."

She didn't mean to speak so emphatically, but surely Angela didn't get it. Holly Hanson was phenomenal. They didn't just hand out awards for cooking if recipes were bad.

"Nikki, you're amazing," Angela said. "You have all the skills to achieve the same success." She watched Nikki, who simply stared at her. She and Holly Hanson weren't even in the same league. How could Angela not see that? "I'm just saying…"

Nikki appreciated the vote of confidence, deciding

to take it for what it was. "Thanks, Ang." Her friend had always believed in her, and Nikki seized on to that knowledge, needing to use it as ammunition for the day's events. "Well, I'll just be happy if I can get a job." She smiled like she was thrilled to be out there, dressed like she was heading to the symphony, practically begging someone to let her cook for them. "Two more interviews to go."

"Good luck," Angela said.

Nikki picked up her mug as she stood. "Thanks."

She couldn't go to an interview—especially this first one at Finique—with only coffee in her stomach. The very idea was laughable. All women everywhere knew that a job interview, whether it was at a restaurant where a very bad breakup had happened or not, required carbs. And in Lakeside, the best place to get properly carbo-loaded was Delucci's Bakery.

Nikki entered the doors to a charming chime from the bell and approached the counter. The smell of freshly baked rolls and breads made her stomach roar. And the espresso—Nikki needed one, stat.

Trish, the owner of the bakery, was one of Nikki's favorite people on the planet. Though she probably got up in the middle of the night to come to work, she greeted everyone like they were old friends.

"Hi, good morning," Nikki said.

Trish, who was more Nikki's mother's age, beamed at her. "Good morning." Her emerald-colored sweater made her eyes seem more green than blue today. "The usual?"

"Yes, please." Nikki felt like she had someone she could confide in here in the city. Her own mother lived so far away, and she hadn't wanted Nikki to come to Lakeside in the first place. So Nikki only told her the good things about her life, reasoning that there was no sense in burdening her parents with the negative. After all, she was sure one of these two upcoming interviews would net her a job.

Trish gave her a conspiratorial look. "Double whip?"

"You know it." Nikki laughed with Trish, the weight of her interview flying away, at least for the moment.

Trish returned a minute later with a mocha latte and reached for the can of whipping cream. She squirted more than a healthy amount on top and handed the to-go cup to Nikki. "So, how's the job search going? Any luck yet?"

"No, no luck." Nikki ignored the twist in her chest. "But I'm trying to stay optimistic. I'm not gonna lie, though. It's pretty hard." She ducked her head and tucked her hair. She was wearing the right clothes today. She'd studied Finique's menu, their hours, and their history listed on their website. She knew everything about the establishment. She'd cooked at five restaurants.

"Well, I have no doubt you'll find a job soon. This is a big city with a lot of hungry people."

Nikki sipped her latte and licked the cream from her top lip. "I hope so. Because if I don't find something soon, I'm going to *be* one of those hungry people." She wanted to believe Trish with all her heart—so she did.

Trish's husband, Marty, emerged from the kitchen in the back, a tray of chocolate-drizzled biscotti in front of him. The smell made Nikki close her eyes and take a deep breath, instantly transporting her straight back to her childhood. Her grandmother had made biscotti for Christmas every year when Nikki was a little girl. Since she didn't drink, she'd taught Nikki to dip the Italian cookies in hot apple cider.

She let the memory play out as Marty set down the tray and reached for a pair of tongs. "Did I hear someone say they were hungry?" He picked up a bag.

"Ooh, fresh biscotti. You know I can't resist that." She couldn't, even if her pocketbook would take a three-dollar hit.

"My father opened these doors with this very recipe." Marty put a fresh cookie in the bag. Nikki started to pull out her wallet, a cute pink thing she'd bought for herself after her Valentine's Day fiasco two years ago.

There was that thought again. Probably because in only a few short weeks, she'd have to experience that day all over again.

Though she could stuff reminders of Valentine's

Day away, she couldn't quite do the same with her memories of Finique. Her heart rate picked up, and she couldn't believe she was even considering stepping foot back inside the restaurant where her heart had been broken. But desperate times called for her to shelve her pride and hope her memories didn't suffocate her when she went to her job interview later that morning.

"No, no, put your money away," Marty said.

Nikki stared at him.

"When you get a job, then we'll let you pay," Trish said, glancing at her husband.

Their generosity touched Nikki's heart. "But—"

"You heard the missus," he said. "And trust me, you don't want to argue with her."

Trish giggled and playfully swatted his arm. "Marty."

Nikki accepted the bag with the biscotti and put her wallet away. "All right. Well, thanks." With both Trish and Marty looking at her with such affection, she inhaled. They believed in her. Angela's words from that morning replayed in Nikki's head.

She could ace this interview. She squared her shoulders and lifted her latte. "Well, I'm off to another job interview. Wish me luck!"

Chapter two

That afternoon, Nikki stood outside of Finique, her heart swimming around in her chest. Here she was again, face-to-face with the very place where the most humiliating breakup of her life had happened.

She remembered the exact table where Ryan had said those horrible words. The precise meal they'd shared. The walk she'd taken back to her apartment, alone.

Gotta go inside, she told herself. She didn't have to dine here, but she did need a job. Badly.

She breathed, strengthened her resolve, and told herself it was going to be fine. Just fine. She stepped down the sidewalk and through the doors. The restaurant wasn't open yet because it was one of those fancy ones that only served dinner.

Everything in front of her was white. White walls. Stark white tables with white chairs. The shelves held glasses and shiny silverware.

A man with dark hair and eyes approached. "Nikki?" The manager wore a pale blue shirt and a posh, striped tie with a suit that probably cost more than her month's rent. He obviously paid attention to his appearance, but he needed to find a new barber because the short, choppy haircut wasn't doing him any favors.

Be nice, she told herself. Only positive thoughts. No judgments on someone's appearance. She knew better than anyone that looks usually only ran skin deep.

"Yes." She flashed him what she hoped was a bright-as-the-sun smile and handed him her resume. He didn't return her grin, and she felt hers slide right off her face.

"This way." He led her to a table smack dab in the middle of the waitstaff preparing the restaurant for opening, and she glanced around nervously.

"It would be such an honor to be a cook here at Finique," she said, her voice just the tiniest bit squeaky. She longed to clear her throat to lower it, but she didn't dare. Finique definitely wasn't a place where people went around clearing their throats. They probably asked for seltzer water for such things.

The manager, who had not introduced himself, looked up from her resume. "Yes. It would." His eyes skated over her, almost like she wasn't worthy of his full attention.

She sat on her hands so she wouldn't fidget. "I ate

here once, and it was one of the best meals of my entire life." She went ahead and did the throat-clearing. No one popped from the immaculate woodwork to arrest her, and the manager continued to stare at her single piece of paper like it was typed in Latin.

"It was Valentine's Day," Nikki said, unsure why she couldn't make herself stop talking. "My boyfriend took me out, and we had the most breathtaking meal." She waited for him to look at her, acknowledge that she was speaking at all. When he didn't, she mentally named him the Silent Supervisor and wished she could yank her resume from his perfectly manicured hands.

"It was a four-course meal with a perfectly paired, peppery zinfandel finished off with the most decadent chocolate soufflé." A giggle burst from her mouth, though there was nothing happy about where this story was going. "Which he ended up dumping me over—which wasn't so good, as you can imagine." She cut her voice off as the Silent Supervisor looked at her like she'd turned green.

Well, the soufflé had been delicious—just not the part where Ryan had ended things while couples around them kissed, got engaged, and made plans for their future.

The Silent Supervisor cleared his throat, but not in the nervous kind of way. More like the I'm-so-much-better-than-you kind of way. Sort of a hoity-toity cough, really.

"But the food was very, very good." Nikki enunciated

each *very* with a hand gesture, as if the Silent Supervisor didn't understand the meaning of the word.

"Your resume doesn't state where you went to culinary school."

Her heart sank all the way to her shoes. "I… I didn't. I'm self-taught." She infused as much confidence into her voice as she could.

The Silent Supervisor seemed to roll his whole upper half, not just his eyes. "Self-taught?"

Nikki nodded, glad the word-vomit about her breakup with Ryan seemed to be over.

"This is Finique, darling." The condescending tone wasn't hard to find. The Silent Supervisor tossed her resume to the table and pushed it back toward her with one finger like it contained a contagious disease. "We don't hire amateurs." He checked his watch as if he had a billion more important things to do.

She lifted her eyebrows, her confidence shot straight through. "Amateurs." She smiled though there wasn't anything to be happy about—anything to keep the anger and hurt from leaking out. The need to get out of this building pressed down on her. "Right. Of course you don't." She picked up her resume with her decade of experience on it. But not the right experience, apparently. "Thank you for your consideration." She stood, her legs conducting her out of this awful restaurant—where now two of the most humiliating experiences of her life had taken place.

She marched down the street, her head held high.

Finique had just lost a customer for life. She hoped they knew that. Sure, maybe she couldn't afford their gourmet dinner prices right now, but someday, when she could, she still wouldn't eat there. And that Silent Supervisor could really use a new haircut.

Vindicated, she headed back over to Delucci's for their day-old bread. They'd graciously agreed to let her have it for free on Wednesdays, as she used it at the community center's daily free meals. Nikki figured if she couldn't get paid to cook, she could still practice her skills, do what she loved, and help some people along the way. She only volunteered twice a week, but it was something.

She pushed into Delucci's even though the sign read CLOSED and found Marty and Trish at the counter, counting out their till.

Marty glanced up at her and picked up a big bag. "Not too much left over today, but here it is."

Nikki took it with a smile, glad her day of interviews was done and she could simply do what she loved most: cook.

"So how'd interview go?" Marty asked, leaning into the counter.

"Marty!" Trish swatted him with a dirty look on her face.

"What?"

"Why do you have to be so nosy?" She looked at Nikki, an apology in her eyes. "I'm sorry."

Nikki forced a giggle out. "No, no, it's okay, he

can ask. But I...I didn't get it." Her shoulders slumped and she had to work to keep her emotions bottled up. She was tired of talking about the job hunt and how she kept getting passed over. Seriously, looking for a job had to be the most demoralizing activity on the planet.

Marty's face fell. "Oh, really. How come?"

She shrugged, her hurt feelings rushing forward again. "Well, aside from going off on a really bad Valentine's Day rant, I don't have a culinary degree, so that disqualifies me. Again." She wouldn't sniff here, just like she wouldn't clear her throat at Finique. Marty and Trish already felt bad for her. Their defeated posture suggested as much. Perhaps she should return to her hometown. She could work at the diner where her mother had waitressed for three decades, live with her parents, get back on her feet. But the thought of leaving Lakeside for a small town hundreds of miles away made her chest ache.

"Don't worry," Marty said. "I know you'll get the next one."

"I just wish I could open my own place, you know?" Nikki sighed and gazed at them like they'd be able to make her dreams come true. "I mean, I know I'm a good cook, but I'm just not good at convincing others I am."

"Well, your food is certainly convincing."

"It sure is, all right."

A flood of gratitude filled her. She picked up the

bag of bread. "Ah, you guys are sweet. Well, thanks again." She made her way out of the bakery and down the bustling street where restaurants, shops, and boutiques all tried to lure customers into their stores with pretty window displays.

A couple of blocks down, she found Gus putting up a FOR SALE sign in the window. Not quite the display she wanted to see, and her mood shifted once again. She knocked on the glass, a hearty smile in place for the man who'd given her enough advice to last a lifetime.

He'd been there on February fourteenth last year, when she was reliving her nightmare from the year before. Gus had given her the task of making a new sandwich for the customers. He didn't know it, but that one thing had kept her from spiraling into a dark place. Creating a sandwich had given her purpose.

He grinned and waved at her, and she did the same. He was branded in her life, and as she walked away, she wished once more that she could afford to buy Gus's building and start her own restaurant.

She arrived at the Lakeside Community Center a few minutes later, the large bag of day-old bread starting to get heavy. With dinner in only an hour, Nikki got to work chopping, dicing, and slicing.

In front of her, more volunteers set up tables and chairs for the anticipated crowd. Wednesdays were notorious for having an unpredictable number of people to feed. Nikki hadn't been volunteering long, but she loved making large quantities of food and setting them up buffet-style for whoever came.

As she put the finishing touches on an almond rice pilaf, she had a brief flash of herself eating here every Wednesday. She really needed a job, and for the first time in years, she'd have to consider other options besides cooking.

Dinner started, distracting her from her personal troubles, and she went out into the crowd after most of the people had been through the line. There was a fantastic turnout tonight, with nearly every chair full and most of the food gone.

She collected an empty basket from one table. "Let me get you some more bread." It did her heart good to be here volunteering instead of lounging at home feeling sorry for herself.

She approached the serving area and spotted Beth, the center's director. A petite woman with red hair she always secured in a bun, Beth wore a smile all the time but used a commanding voice when giving directions. Nikki had never known anyone to disobey her.

"Wow, such a big turnout today, huh?" Nikki eyed the bin of Valentine's Day decorations in Beth's hands.

She set them in an empty spot at the end of the paper goods table. "Well, that's because you're here."

"Uh, what?" Nikki cocked her hip as she lifted her eyebrows.

"People love your cooking. Once word got out that you volunteer here on Wednesdays, everyone comes. You're like a rock star chef to those in need." She beamed at Nikki like she'd solved world hunger singlehandedly. All she'd done was make some chicken.

A well of resentment opened up in her soul. "Well, at least someone appreciates my cooking." She had a hard time keeping her voice even, and she dropped her gaze to the gaudy Valentine's Day items in the bin. The roses looked like a giant had sat on them. "Wow, Valentine's Day already, huh?"

Beth beamed into the offending box of red and pink. "Yeah it's coming up." She sighed. "I think we'll get some volunteers to help us decorate once we're done."

"Count me in." Even though Nikki would rather not celebrate Valentine's Day in any way, her alternative was going home to an empty apartment and waiting up for Angela so they could talk about Holly Hanson's. Again.

"Okay." Beth pulled out the smashed roses, and Nikki took that as her cue to get the breadbasket refilled the way she'd said she would.

The next afternoon, Nikki couldn't avoid her situation any longer. She fired up the laptop and got herself over to an online job board. Her second love was dogs, and she found a dog walker position in only a few minutes.

The sound of Angela's footsteps came closer as she

left her bedroom and entered the kitchen. "What are you doing?" She looked at the computer screen and then Nikki for an explanation.

Nikki turned from the bar where she'd been doing her job research. "Well, given that my job hunting isn't going so well, I figured I might need to get a 'day job,' so to speak." She twisted her fingers together the way she did when her nerves got the better of her.

Angela finished securing her dark hair in a ponytail. "A day job?" She wore her black work pants and a white shirt, which contrasted with her dark skin. Nikki couldn't escape her friend's light green eyes, and a little flutter stole through her stomach.

"Yeah, you know, something where I can earn a paycheck while I continue to search for my dream job." She waved her hands like there were birds flying through the apartment. She consciously lowered them to her sides. "And since I'm pretty good with dogs, I figured maybe...I could be a dog walker?" Why she'd framed the last part of her sentence as a question, she wasn't sure. Maybe because she wasn't sure about anything in her life right now.

"Nikki, you can't just give up."

"I'm not giving up," she assured Angela. "I'm just considering other options. I've got to pay the rent somehow."

Angela moved over to the kitchen table where her purse sat and pulled out her keys. "Well, I wish I could help you out. I'm just not making the kind of tips I thought I would."

Nikki cocked her head, concerned about her friend. "Bad tippers at a place like Holly Hanson's?" That made no sense. Men like the Silent Supervisor went there...oh, wait. Actually, Nikki couldn't see him leaving that great of tip. But still. Even fifteen percent of a hundred-dollar ticket was good money.

Angela shouldered her purse. "No, the tips are fine. There's just not enough of them. Business is down."

"Oh, that's too bad. And surprising."

"Hey, if you don't have any plans later, maybe you could come by at closing, grab a glass of wine?"

Nikki shook her head, her face scrunching into a distasteful grimace.

But Angela wouldn't be deterred, and she knew where to hit Nikki hard. "If Holly's there, maybe I can introduce you."

"Really?" Nikki wasn't sure what she'd say to the woman, but the possibility of meeting her was too exciting to pass up.

"Yeah, I mean, considering you idolize her, maybe you might want to meet her?"

"Yeah, absolutely." She edged forward a little. "I just hope I don't make a fool of myself and start to ramble."

Angela remained straight-faced as she shook her head. "No, I can't imagine that," she said with more sarcasm in her voice than actual air.

Nikki scoffed as she rolled her eyes. "Oh yeah?"

"Okay, I can imagine it a little bit. But that's why we love you! I'll see you at ten."

"Mm-hm." Nikki nodded her head in short, little bursts as Angela walked out. She turned back to her laptop, which still showed the cute little pug that needed a dog walker. "Okay."

She exhaled, but her enthusiasm for staying up until ten didn't wane. Her eyes traveled to the cookbook she'd be cooking dinner from that night.

Holly Brings the Heat! sat there, and Nikki's smile grew at the same rate as her anxiety. "Holly Hanson," she whispered.

She whipped around and went into the bathroom. She looked at her own face and practiced not saying anything. She counted to ten, thinking about Holly's fiesta tacos she'd cooked last week.

Nothing came out of her mouth.

She could do this. Satisfied that she wouldn't be a rambling, bumbling fool that night with her idol chef, she went back into the kitchen and paged through the cookbook, looking for something that would take a couple of hours. Anything to distract her from thinking of possible conversation topics.

Chapter three

Paul Delucci took a bite of the *cassoulet* and cringed. He'd followed the recipe exactly, the same way he always did. But the pork barely tasted like anything, and the white beans simply felt like mush in his mouth. Not exactly pleasing.

It was no wonder the kitchen had been slow for a couple of months now—maybe longer. If he could just get Holly to listen…

But Paul wasn't extraordinarily gifted at getting the other adults in his life to listen to him. His own rift with his parents proved that, and no matter how many times he'd tried to explain to his father that he didn't have a superiority complex, his dad still thought he did.

The three other chefs in the kitchen went about their business, washing tomatoes, prepping desserts, and putting up appetizers.

The sound of Holly's four-inch heels clicking

on the tile alerted Paul, and he stepped around the counter to intercept her. "Holly, a moment."

She complied, though she certainly wasn't happy about it. Brushing back her brown hair highlighted with blonde, Holly glared at him with her sharp, hazel eyes. "What now?"

"The *cassoulet*," he said, squinting at her. She remained blank-faced, as if he hadn't mentioned this to her last night.

He backed up a step and folded his arms, ready to get into the fray with her again. "Look, Holly, all I'm saying is that you need to try it. The recipe needs to be tweaked."

She stared at him, and if he hadn't been working with her for five years, he might have backed down. Lots of other chefs had come and gone over the time he'd been at Holly Hanson's, but he'd stayed.

"I don't need to try it," she said. "It's my recipe."

"I understand what you're saying. I'm just a little confused." He sighed. The banging of dishes and the hiss from the stove behind him mirrored how he felt inside. "Look, all I'm saying is that we need to come up with a solution to the problem."

"And what is the problem?"

Paul could name any number of things. The empty tables. The waitresses complaining that they weren't making enough to pay their bills. The mysterious, late-night meetings Holly had with her investors.

He chose to go with, "The *cassoulet*. Have you tried it?" He'd asked her to please just taste it. If it was going to sit at the top of their menu as their chef's special, it should be the most outstanding dish leaving the kitchen. In Paul's opinion, it was one of the worst. But he wasn't Holly Hanson. It wasn't his name on the door or the paychecks. If he wanted to change a recipe, he needed her permission.

But he couldn't even get her to see the problem.

She rocked back on her heels. "I know what it tastes like."

"I don't think that you do. Because the recipe is bland." There, he'd said it.

She scoffed, her mind completely closed. "Bland?"

"Yeah."

She gritted her teeth, and her mouth barely moved when she said, "Perhaps the problem lies with my executive chef, who is unable to execute my recipe properly."

He kept his arms cinched across his black chef's jacket, a frustrated chuckle leaving his lips. "Well, your executive chef respectfully disagrees." Honestly, talking to her felt exactly like trying to explain to his father that while baking was a wonderful thing, Paul wanted to do more than make bread and cookies.

Why didn't anyone hear him? He was speaking English, wasn't he?

Holly's head bounced as she gave him a bit of attitude. "I believe my name is on the front door. So would you please stop arguing with me and do as I say?"

Paul pressed his mouth into a thin line and dropped his gaze to the floor. He wasn't going to get her to admit anything, not right now—maybe not ever. He nodded once, his anger rising to the top of his head, where he released it. No sense in being upset about something he couldn't control.

"Are we good?" Holly asked.

He flicked his eyes toward hers. "Yes, Chef," he said in a loud voice.

"Thank you," she whispered before striding away—as much as her high heels and sleek pencil skirt would allow her to stride.

Paul went back to overseeing the kitchen, which ran without a hitch. The *cassoulet* just needed…something to make it sparkle again. If it were up to him, he'd add more garlic—maybe another whole clove—and a splash of heat. Maybe not Tabasco sauce, but perhaps sriracha would give the dish the oomph it needed.

Oh, and he'd cook it longer to get the ragout flavors really deep before adding the beans. But it would take a miracle to get Holly to listen to him.

Nikki felt like she was walking through the pearly gates when she entered Holly Hanson's. The atmosphere was everything she'd hoped it would be, though she did notice that many of the tables sat empty.

A smile accompanied her slow steps as she took in the grandeur of the restaurant. The low lighting, the high bar, the swanky music… It all made her want to grab a dish of the chef's special and curl up in a back booth.

She took off her coat as she advanced farther into the restaurant, glancing around for Angela. She spotted her after only a few steps.

"Hey," Angela said, sidling over to her with a payment billfold in her hand.

"Hey." Nikki exhaled, her nerves no calmer now than they'd been hours ago. Apparently, making spicy chicken teriyaki bowls had not given her the distraction she'd needed from meeting Holly.

"You made it." Angela tipped a smile at Nikki.

"I did indeed." She couldn't help the awed quality of her voice. "Wow, just look at this place."

Angela glanced around but didn't seem that impressed. "Yep. Listen, give me a minute. Why don't you go wait by the bar?" She leaned in closer. "And check out the cute bartender. Definitely my type." She gave the tall man behind the bar a smile as she walked away. Nikki chuckled before turning to hang her coat on a hook.

Her stomach felt like she'd swallowed a hive of bees, and she ran her palm down the front of her pink blouse, hoping she would be calm once Holly made an appearance. She took a seat near the end of the bar, and the bartender came closer.

She could see why Angela liked him. Dark cocoa-colored skin. Beautiful eyes. Square jaw. Clean-cut and employed. What wasn't to like?

He put a napkin on the bar in front of her. "Hi."

"Hi."

"What can I get you?"

"Glass of red wine, please."

"House, or would you like to see the wine list?"

"Uh—"

Angela appeared in the empty seat next to Nikki, her flirtatious smile set on high. "Maybe you could pick out something special for her from the list? This is my best friend, Nikki."

Nikki raised her hand in a friendly wave, but she didn't look away from Angela. She hadn't seen her friend this enamored with a man in...well, ever.

"Nikki, this is Jerrod."

"Hi."

"Nice to meet you."

"Same."

Jerrod ducked his head in an adorable way and moved down the bar to get Nikki's drink. She turned toward Angela, her curiosity spilling over. "How come you've never mentioned him before?"

Angela watched him work. "Oh, because there's no future there." She shook her head and met Nikki's eyes.

"He has a girlfriend or something?"

"No." She lifted one shoulder in a baby shrug. "But apparently, Holly frowns upon her employees dating."

Nikki scoffed and laughed. Though Holly could do no wrong in the kitchen, that policy seemed pretty ridiculous. If something like that had happened where her mother had worked, she wouldn't have met Nikki's father. She watched Angela go back out onto the floor to drop off a ticket, put on her smile, and get back to work.

Her mind drifted to little old Cedar Hills, a few hours south of Lakeside. Her mother had been a waitress at a quaint diner, and she'd met Nikki's dad as he came to the restaurant with their supply of produce. They'd fallen in love, and the rest was history.

Nikki sighed. She wished all romances were so easy, but the fact that she still hadn't met Mr. Right certainly testified otherwise.

Jerrod returned, bearing a lot more than a wine glass. "Here you are. Enjoy." He placed a red casserole dish in front of her with a roll of silverware inside a black napkin.

Nikki glanced at the food. "Uh, a *cassoulet*?"

"Tonight's special. On the house." He grinned at her.

"Wow, thanks."

He moved away, leaving her to experience the food with her eyes and nose first. After unwrapping her napkin, she placed it in her lap, eager to taste Holly's recipe. Nikki picked up her fork and fixed a delicate bite of pork and beans. She lifted the utensil to her nose and sniffed.

The smell of salty pork with a hint of garlic made

her eyes roll back in her head. It wasn't every day that she got to eat at such a high-end restaurant.

She put the food in her mouth, and her eyes snapped open. The smile left her face, and she glanced around, almost embarrassed, to check if anyone had seen her reaction. No one seemed to be paying her any attention, and Jerrod lingered at the opposite end of the bar.

Glancing down at the *cassoulet*, Nikki couldn't believe it had tasted so…bland. It wasn't good. It wasn't bad. It was like nothing, which in her opinion, was so much worse. At least bad food tasted like something.

She put her fork down, utterly disappointed. She hoped when she came face-to-face with the celebrity chef that Angela wouldn't be right about her being a diva.

But no matter what, she couldn't take another bite of that *cassoulet*. She lifted her wine glass to her lips to wash down the little bit she'd consumed.

Chapter Four

P aul asked his sous chefs to get the kitchen cleaned and everything put away for the night. His frustration had only grown as the hours had passed, and he needed a break from this business. He'd known how rough it could be going in—he'd worked at the bakery with his father long enough to experience that. The day started early at the bakery, but it ended well past midnight for Paul.

It seemed that he and his father were always on opposite ends of the spectrum.

He changed out of his chef's jacket and pulled a long-sleeved shirt over his head. He didn't want to eat at Holly's, but a drink sounded great. After a day like today, he deserved it.

He walked through the restaurant and the few lingering customers to the bar, where a seat remained at the end beside a pretty auburn-haired woman wearing a frilly pink top.

Jerrod caught sight of him and waved. Paul liked the bartender, and they'd started spending some time together outside of work. Paul didn't usually do that because he didn't have time. And he didn't want to be buddy-buddy with his sous chef or his pastry chef. It was very lonely as the executive chef, but Paul had never really minded until a few months ago.

So when Jerrod had run into Paul at the rec center, they'd played basketball together. They'd started doing that more and more, and Paul could really use a friendly face tonight.

"Hey," Paul said as he eased his tired body onto the barstool.

"What's it tonight?"

Paul smiled, though nothing about tonight warranted such an action. "Oh, something that pairs with frustration."

Jerrod gave him a knowing smile. "Got it."

The woman next to him smelled like strawberries, roses, and other red things. He tried not to look at her too quickly, but he turned that way anyway. He noticed her wide, innocent eyes in a peculiar shade of brown. They pulled at him and wouldn't let go.

Her hair shone with some dark notes, too, and he wondered what color it would be in natural light. She was dressed well, wore makeup, and that scent...

He smiled at her, his eyes falling to the bar—where a bowl of *cassoulet* sat. His heart pumped out an extra beat, and he was suddenly anxious to know what she thought of it. "See you have the special. How was it?"

The woman, who had been nodding and smiling, faced the bar again, her grin fading. "Uh…it was, uh. It was okay." She turned toward him, her loose curls falling over her shoulder. The grin appeared, and it lit something in him that had been dormant for a while. "I just wasn't that hungry."

She was also not that great at lying. "But you got to try it, at least, right?" He gestured toward it as if she hadn't noticed the bowl in front of her. He watched her face for a reaction.

"Mm-hm, yeah. I did."

And the bowl was still full. He couldn't help himself. Maybe if he had some real customer feedback, Holly would listen. Or maybe he just liked the way this woman's voice sounded and he wanted to keep talking to her. No matter what, he asked, "Did you like it?"

"Oh, um." Her voice was barely audible above the elevator music wafting down from the speakers in the ceiling. She actually looked over her shoulder to see if anyone was lingering nearby. "Yeah, I'd pass, maybe. Try something else, perhaps." She giggled and nodded like they'd just shared a secret with each other.

He'd been watching her, but now he dropped his gaze to the bar. A quick half-laugh left his lips. "What was it about it that you didn't like?"

She stared at the bowl of offending *cassoulet*. "It

was just a little bland. I think it needed something. I don't know."

Though he had used the exact same word—bland—to describe the *cassoulet*, his pride was taking a serious hit here.

He picked up his glass and swirled his wine. "Good to know." He took a sip, wishing his emotions weren't quite so at war with each other. Would he have liked her more if she'd enjoyed a *cassoulet* he knew was inferior? He should be grateful she seemed to possess a discerning palate. It wasn't like she'd tasted and then critiqued *his* recipe.

She turned back to him, leaned in, and whispered, "You know, frankly, I'm a little surprised."

Paul was, too. Holly had been slipping for months, and he didn't know why. He set his wine glass on the counter and worked hard to school his features before he looked at her. "It was that bad?"

"No, it's just..." Her denial came quickly, and she considered the bowl of food again. She scrunched up her lips in a cute way that Paul wished he didn't find quite so attractive. "It could've used something to... pizzazz it up, you know? It just wasn't—it didn't really have that 'wow factor' that I was expecting."

Paul nodded though he wasn't sure what she meant. "The 'wow factor.'" He couldn't help the twinge of annoyance in his chest, though her assessment of the *cassoulet* was spot-on.

The woman nodded, a little too emphatically, in

his opinion. "You know, Holly probably just needs a new executive chef or something. That's what I'm thinking." She gave him a wide-eyed look like her word would become law.

Paul gave a single nod in slow motion. A smile came to his lips, but it wasn't exactly happy—more like he was trying to figure out what she'd just said and why it felt like she'd stabbed him in the heart with a fork. All four tines of a fork.

"Sounds like you eat out a lot," he said, his voice miraculously even.

She obviously mistook his smile for friendliness. "No, no. I—I, uh, just know a lot about food." She didn't seem bothered by what she'd said, and of course, she had no idea who she'd said it to. She grinned at him, and his frustration edged up a notch because he actually found her honesty and innocence so attractive.

"Of course you do. Because...you eat food." The smile on his face felt manic, stretched too far. "Everyone's a food critic these days." He laughed a couple of times and wanted to drown this day in his glass of red wine.

"Oh no. I'm not a food critic. Actually, a lot of people think that I am. I was at the grocery store last week..." She trailed off, for which Paul was grateful.

He struggled to hide his exhaustion and his irritation with Holly, and he couldn't camouflage his feelings for much longer. When she asked, "I'm sorry, did I say something to upset you?" he knew he hadn't hidden them well at all.

He exhaled, the tension leaving his shoulders. What would telling her who he was accomplish? Nothing. She didn't seem like Holly, and maybe she would listen to him, but after the day he'd already had, he decided revealing who he was—the very executive chef she'd just suggested firing—wasn't worth the conversation.

So she was pretty. She had a good air about her. She knew food. But she also thought he should be replaced, and though he'd never feared for his job here, he suddenly did.

"No," he finally said in response to her question. "No, I just, uh, I just got some bad news tonight." He couldn't find a reason to make her feel embarrassed that she'd insulted him.

"Oh, sorry." She seemed genuine, too, even if she turned back to her pathetic bowl of *cassoulet* a moment later. "Well, if it makes you feel better, I'm sure your news isn't as bad as the feedback they're getting on this *cassoulet.*" She gave him a flirtatious smile, and Paul had no other choice but to laugh.

She giggled with him, longer and with more volume. He needed to get out of there. Even though he agreed with her and wanted to change the recipe, his defenses still battled with what she'd said. After all, she'd just bashed his cooking.

Not my recipe, though.

He eased away from the bar while her laughter

still rang in his ears. "Have a good night." He made it to the exit before he turned back to look at her. She slouched against the barstool, clearly a bit flummoxed as to what had just happened.

Paul wasn't, though. Her opinion of the *cassoulet* was his, too. And he needed to do something about it.

Nikki wished Angela had told her to come at eleven o'clock instead of ten. Customers lingered, and while she usually left when a restaurant closed, the possibility of meeting Holly still dangled on the horizon, an opportunity she couldn't pass up.

Angela disappeared into the kitchen and didn't return. Nikki wasn't sure how long she was supposed to wait, and she waved off more wine from Jerrod. Her gaze landed on the vacant seat next to her where that man had sat.

She'd definitely said something to upset him, and regret stole through her. What if what she'd said about the *cassoulet* got back to Angela, or worse, Holly Hanson herself?

Nikki shouldn't have mentioned anything. Her and her babbling mouth. For once, she'd like her flapping lips to get her something good instead of landing her in trouble.

She thought about the man and his perfectly symmetrical face, his bright blue eyes, and his close-cut hair. He was handsome and tall, and Nikki regretted complaining about the food all over again. Just her luck that he'd probably enjoyed the *cassoulet*...if that was even possible.

She glanced up, realizing that Jerrod had taken her glass and left the bar. In fact, she was the only one remaining in the restaurant. I should go, she thought, her stomach quivering the tiniest bit. *Not gonna meet Holly tonight.*

She'd twisted to reach for her coat when she heard someone say, "We can just talk in here."

Nikki turned, everything inside her freezing when she saw the tall, beautiful, and glamorous Holly Hanson walking along the opposite wall and entering the dining room. A wall hid Nikki, still sitting at the bar, but the dining room wasn't soundproof.

A man came with Holly, well dressed with dark hair and a somewhat disgusted look on his face. "If you're afraid that I'm gonna see what your office looks like, it's a little late, Holly. I've already seen it." He definitely didn't sound happy, and Nikki wished she could make herself invisible and get out of the restaurant.

"Oh, I just have to catch up on some of that paperwork." Holly tacked on a laugh that sounded a bit on the nervous side.

"There's a pile of paperwork in your office that looks like Mount Everest. What happened to your assistant?" The voices came from directly behind

Nikki, so she couldn't see them, but the annoyance in the man's voice wasn't hard to hear, even around the divider.

"She quit."

He sighed heavily. "So did the last three. Holly, listen, you need to hire someone to organize all of this. Now, I've been asking for the financials for months, and as your investor, I'm entitled to see them on a regular basis."

"I just don't think you understand. I'm not just running this restaurant. I am overseeing my entire brand." Holly sounded on the prouder side of herself, and Nikki wondered if Angela could be right about her. Still, it seemed like she was being reprimanded, and Nikki didn't want to hear all of this. But how could she get up now?

"Exactly. And that's the problem. You need to focus and pay attention to the restaurant."

"I completely revamped the menu six months ago—at your request."

"No, what you did was, you pulled out some of your older signature dishes instead of creating new ones. And I have to be honest with you, I don't think this place is going to survive with just the status quo."

Holly Hanson's was going to go out of business? How was that even possible? Nikki really wanted to go see if this guy was like that uppity manager at Finique—though he seemed to have plenty to say as he continued with, "Look, please just get me the paperwork soon so I can dig through all this and see how bad things really are. I'll see myself out."

Footsteps sounded as he made his way to the front door. Nikki caught a glimpse of his back as he turned the handle. The distinct sound of heel steps on tile came toward her.

She froze. Dread and horror choked her, and that invisibility would've been great about now.

"Oh, uh." An anxiety-ridden giggle escaped her throat.

Holly glanced up and stopped as Nikki turned and came face-to-face with her idol chef.

"Hi. I'm so sorry." She held up one hand in a placating gesture. "I didn't mean to be a fly on the wall." She gestured toward the dividing wall between her and the room where Holly had just been chewed out. And why couldn't she stop smiling?

Holly stared at her, her gaze sharp. Nikki wondered how she'd achieved so many genius recipes so quickly. Trying to focus, she said, "But I—I guess you two didn't see me sitting here when you came in, so I just—I didn't know what to do exactly. So…"

Holly squinted at her. "A cough would have been the polite thing to do."

"You're absolutely right," Nikki agreed instantly, an idea occurring to her. All she needed was a few more seconds of bravery—and maybe some of her ability to babble.

"Listen, I—I couldn't help overhearing your

conversation, and the fact that you need a new assistant." She stood and faced Holly fully, her hope rising like a helium balloon.

Holly shook her head as if annoyed and blinked a couple of times. "I'm sorry. You are?"

Nikki lunged one step forward and then reminded herself to not appear so enthusiastic. Still, when she said, "Nikki," and grabbed onto Holly's hand to shake it, she was definitely the most eager beaver in town. Even when Holly pulled her hand back and grimaced, Nikki continued. "Um, I'm Angela's friend."

When Holly stared at her, Nikki clarified. "Um, Angela, your server?"

"Oh, yes. Yes, the new girl."

Nikki wondered how Holly didn't know all of her employees, new or not. "Mm-hm. Anyhow, I don't mean to be intrusive, but I just happen to be looking for a job." When Holly didn't roll her eyes or walk away, Nikki's confidence grew.

Keep babbling, baby.

"And I'm very experienced in the restaurant industry, and it would be a privilege to work for you. That is, if you're hiring, of course."

Holly seemed to be wearing a mask, and it wasn't a smiling one. "Do you know who I am?"

"Oh! Yes, of course, I do! Actually, it's kind of embarrassing to admit, but I think I own every single cookbook that you've ever published."

Holly's eyebrows went up. Finally! A reaction.

"Which is why it would mean so much to me to work for you." Nikki closed her mouth, hoping her babbling about the cookbooks and the privilege-to-work-for-you tactic had worked.

"What did you say your name is, sweetheart?"

"Nikki. Nikki Turner." She wondered how long it would take for Holly to remember her name.

"And you've done office work?"

Nikki's smile faded, and her eyes darted away. "Office work?" Her head started bobbing of its own free will. "Yeah, uh, yeah of course. Did I mention I'm available to start right away?" She inhaled, smiled, and nodded again.

You're not a bobble-head. Stop nodding!

Holly raised one eyebrow and circled Nikki, sizing her up. She paused at Nikki's side. "Criminal record?"

"No." Holly took another step, and Nikki twisted with her. "Although, I did get a parking ticket once."

Holly spun back to her, a sharp look on her face.

"But I—I paid it immediately. Mm-hm." Nikki nodded, silently begging a paid parking ticket to be satisfactory to Holly.

She pointed at Nikki before moving around the bar to get a drink. "And Angela will vouch for you? Right?"

"Yes! Definitely! Mm-hm. Hundred percent."

Holly lifted a tumbler and a container of Scotch. "Well, I am desperate…"

Nikki's insides did a little dance. "Uh, does that mean that I'm hired?"

Putting the bottle down, Holly met Nikki's eyes, her unmoving mask back in place. "Meet me tomorrow at noon."

Nikki nodded, her breath coming so shallowly she couldn't quite form a single word.

"And that conversation you just eavesdropped on…"

Nikki shook her head. "Doesn't leave the room. Ever." She smiled, but Holly simply lifted her drink to her lips, as if everything she said to everyone was always obeyed.

"Okay, well, I'm gonna, uh—the exit's this way. You look beautiful, by the way." Nikki hurried toward the door, hoping with every step that Holly wouldn't call her back and say she'd changed her mind. Once on the street, she released the air that had been accumulating in her lungs.

She didn't dare even look through the window to see if Holly still stood at the bar, watching.

Half a block down the street, Nikki allowed a small squeal to rise through her throat. "I got a job!" she exclaimed to the red light. It didn't answer back. But she didn't care.

She'd just gotten a job at Holly Hanson's, and she knew this was going to be the start of something great.

Chapter Five

Nikki gave herself the luxury of sleeping in the following day. After all, she didn't have to be at work until noon.

She rolled over and smiled. Work. She had work.

Because of her new job, she didn't make it into Delucci's until much later than she normally did. She had a feeling working with Holly would require a lot of caffeine, but she certainly hadn't seemed like diva material.

She pushed inside the bakery, inhaling the yeasty smell of fresh bread and the distinct scent of coffee and sugar. A smile rushed to her face, and everything in the world seemed absolutely right.

It didn't matter that she'd gone without working or that Valentine's Day was right around the corner. She had a job now, and her future was nothing but bright, man or no man come February fourteenth.

Trish and Marty both worked behind the counter,

of course. They came in early in the morning and stayed until afternoon, and she marveled at their strength and tenacity. She stepped up to the counter and greeted them.

"So how come so late today?" Marty asked, finishing up with a customer. He wore a pine tree-colored sweater slightly dusted with flour, and Nikki grinned at him.

"Oh, I got a job! But I don't start until noon."

Trish wiped her hands on her apron. "Oh, that's great news! Congratulations." Her smile couldn't have been more genuine, and Nikki reminded herself to call her parents and tell them about the job, too.

Marty leaned forward. "So you'll be cooking again?"

"Oh, well, not exactly," Nikki said. "I mean, I'm working in a restaurant, but I'll be doing office work, so…" She didn't want to downplay the work, and yes, she'd rather be cooking, but if Finique wouldn't hire her because of her lack of a culinary degree, she had no chance at Holly Hanson's.

"Oh, there's nothing wrong with that," Trish said, buoying Nikki's spirits.

"The best part about it is, I'll be working for a top chef that can teach me the ins and outs of business." Nikki didn't mean to sound so proud of herself, but she had babbled her way into the job, and it was Holly Hanson…

"That is a smart move," Trish said.

"So who is this top chef?" Marty asked.

"Holly. Hanson." Nikki giggled, sure they'd leap across the counter and dance with her.

Instead, they looked at each other with disbelief in their eyes. Trish exhaled heavily, her smile gone completely.

Confusion raced through Nikki, but thoughts of the *cassoulet* quelled the feeling. They probably thought Holly couldn't teach her anything.

"Have you eaten at her restaurant before?" she asked.

Trish pressed one palm to her heart while Marty seemed fascinated by the biscotti. "Well, we know who she is."

Nikki glanced down at her phone. The clock ticked closer and closer to noon. "Oh my gosh. I'm so late. I gotta go." She secured her purse on her shoulder.

"Oh! Don't forget your coffee." Trish handed it to Nikki.

Flustered, she took it. "Right, okay. Thanks. Bye!" She ran out of the bakery, fumbling with her umbrella to get it open. Rain fell in a steady drizzle, and she couldn't show up at Holly's with frizzy hair. She finally got the umbrella up and transferred her coffee to her other hand as her phone chimed.

She took quick, short steps in her heels, hoping she was dressed appropriately for Holly, who'd been wearing a designer skirt and blouse, heels, and perfect makeup at close to midnight the previous evening.

She managed to type out a text to her mom with only one thumb. *I got a job! I'll call you tonight and tell you about it.*

She took a sip of coffee, almost spilling it down her face as she tried to juggle her purse, her umbrella, the phone, and the coffee.

Can't wait, her mom texted back, and Nikki grinned at her phone.

She was nearly to Holly's. And she wasn't going to be late. Satisfaction slipped through her as she put her phone in her purse.

She glanced up only half a second before she was about to run into a very tall object. A very tall object that turned out to be a very handsome man. A very handsome man that her coffee drenched as she came to a screeching stop.

"Oh!" She stared at the huge, spreading stain on his light blue shirt. Then she looked into the face of the man who'd sat next to her at the bar last night.

Paul jumped back as if he could escape the coffee that had already stained his shirt. Irritation sprang into his mind, and he wondered where the phone he'd been looking at had gone.

"Oh my gosh, your shirt! I'm so sorry." The *cassoulet* woman looked at him, and the moment she recognized him wasn't hard to miss. Her beautiful brown eyes widened, and her mouth dropped. "You?" Horror washed over her face, and she struggled to put her umbrella down.

Paul's smile was born of both gladness at seeing her again and exasperation as he glanced at his ruined clothes. "Well, well. If it isn't the food critic from the other night." He flicked his hand to rid it of the sticky coffee.

"My apologizes. But I'm just running late, and I'm—I'm a—a little frazzled." She circled him in a dance, and he turned back to her.

"I can see that."

Her feet wouldn't stop moving, and Paul kept shuffling lest she had something else to throw at him. He checked his shirt again, but it was a hopeless mess.

She sighed and shook her head, clearly unsure what to do. "Uh, look, if you're here for dinner, I don't think they open for a few hours."

She seemed apologetic about that, but he just wanted to get inside and try to figure out why he simultaneously wanted her to stay close but also get far away. He searched his pocket for his keys, but he couldn't find them. "Thanks. I'm well aware of the hours." Where were his blasted keys? "And you're waiting for…"

Before the woman could answer, Holly approached wearing her designer coat and a white scarf. "Good, I'm glad you're here, Paul." She stood back an extra step, and Paul didn't miss the horrified look on the other woman's face.

"Go ahead, open the door," Holly said. "I guess you guys have met?"

Paul finally located his keys. "Is there any reason why we should have?" Everything was happening so fast, but he fitted the key into the lock. If he could just get inside, get back to his kitchen, everything would be fine. He'd already resolved not to pick a fight with Holly about her recipes today. He just wanted to cook.

"Uh, yes, this is my new assistant," Holly said, the words entering Paul's ears but not making much sense.

"What is your name?" Holly asked the other woman, and Paul watched her, too.

"Nikki." She said it a little emphatically, in Paul's opinion, but he also knew it took Holly an extraordinarily long time to remember names.

"Nikki. Nikki, this is Paul, my executive chef."

And now she knew. She knew she'd insulted him last night, spilled coffee on him this morning, and tried to instruct him about the hours of the restaurant where he'd cooked for five years.

Pure panic poured through her expression. A healthy blush colored her face, and Paul ducked his head so she wouldn't have to experience any more humiliation than necessary.

Holly grabbed the flap of his jacket and examined his shirt. He glanced down too, realizing he'd have to work the next twelve hours in a damp, coffee-stained shirt.

"For God's sake, Paul, can't you wear a clean shirt to work?" Holly gave him a dirty look and entered the restaurant, leaving Paul standing on the sidewalk with the reason for his predicament.

He looked at Nikki, and she stared back, clearly upset and not knowing what to do about any of it. It had been a long time since he'd been out with a woman, but something stirred within him, and he wondered if she might be worth the trouble of an unintended insult and a stained shirt.

She finally drew a deep breath and followed Holly. Paul waved at nothing, sighed, and had no choice but to get to work, coffee stains, beautiful women, and all.

Chapter Six

Nikki had never been so mortified. Even when Ryan had ended their relationship on Valentine's Day and abandoned her to walk home alone. Even when she'd babbled about the encounter to the Silent Supervisor. Even when she'd been caught eavesdropping on a very private conversation.

No, none of those came close to telling the executive chef of a five-star restaurant—who surely had a culinary degree—that he needed to be replaced.

You didn't know it was him, she told herself as she followed Holly through the restaurant. But that didn't matter. She shouldn't have said anything, and once again, her tongue had gotten her in trouble.

The scent of coffee and cologne followed her, the smell belonging to Paul and infusing every breath she took. She wished he wasn't quite so good looking. Didn't smell quite so delicious. Didn't work here as the executive chef.

Holly opened the door to her office, and all of Nikki's problems about Paul disappeared. She'd never seen anything like this. The restaurant, with its custom furniture and low lighting, was without a single fork out of place. Holly's office was the antithesis of that.

A wall supported three filing cabinets, and on top of those sat more filing boxes in green and blue. Several metal shelving units held more boxes, and Nikki saw another cabinet and a tall stand of lockers—which she really hoped didn't contain paper of any kind—beside Holly's desk.

It was an absolute mess. And shining in the middle of all of it stood a black bookshelf with several gold trophies.

"Well, here we are." Holly paused at her desk and set her purse down. "Uh, you can put your things over there."

"Okay." Nikki moved behind her and hung her purse on a hook.

"And, uh, oh. Before we start, I need for you to pick up my dry cleaning." Holly handed her a pick-up slip.

Nikki just stared at it. "Oh, uh—"

"And when you get back, I'll have a couple of other errands for you to run."

This wasn't exactly what Nikki had expected, but then again, she hadn't known what to expect. "Okay, sure. Absolutely." She glanced at the dry cleaning slip.

"Whatever you need." She re-zipped her coat, as she'd apparently be wearing it for a while longer.

After she'd walked the three blocks to the dry cleaner and the three blocks back to the restaurant, Nikki lamented her choice of footwear. Holly promptly sent her to the bank, the post office, and finally, to take her car through the car wash.

It was still raining, so Nikki really didn't know what the point of washing the car was. But Holly wanted it done, so Nikki did it.

Finally, Holly taught her how to get on the computer, where the files were, and gave her a few folders with papers to input. Nikki was used to working long hours on her feet but quickly learned that hours behind a desk came with its own set of problems.

Just before the restaurant opened, she stood and worked the kinks out of her shoulders and neck. She had not properly carbo-loaded or caffeinated for this day. She went out to the restaurant and poured herself a cup of coffee.

She'd no sooner taken one sip and turned when Paul approached, wearing a black chef's coat and a black-and-white striped apron around his trim waist. Her heart pumped out an extra beat.

"Whoa. Danger! Lady with a coffee coming through." He held up both hands and gave her a winning smile that showed off his white teeth.

Instant foolishness filled her. "Do you want some?"

"Yeah, as long as it's in a cup and not down my

shirt." He gestured to his chest, and Nikki had no choice but to notice how tall he was, how broad his shoulders spanned, and how snugly his clothes fit.

"Right." Nikki turned to pour him a cup of coffee, telling herself he was off-limits. Number one, she'd insulted him right to his face. Number two, Angela had said Holly didn't allow her employees to date. Still, she remembered that he'd gotten bad news last night, and he'd still been kind to her in the same moment she was insulting him. She glanced over her shoulder. "How come you didn't tell me who you were last night?"

"Somehow, I doubt that would have stopped you from speaking your mind." He wore a playful smile when she turned.

"You're probably right." If she was going to work with this man, they needed to get along. It seemed like he'd already forgiven her for the slight against his food, and she smiled at him. "But at least I wouldn't have put my foot in my mouth."

Paul didn't seem annoyed today, though he had been last night. He'd tried to hide it, but Nikki had noticed. He took a deep breath as his smile faded. "Truth is, you were right about the *cassoulet*. It was bland."

Nikki was about to protest when Holly stepped right between them. She looked at Paul, her stone-faced mask in place. "Nikki, come with me."

It was impossible to know if she was in trouble or not. Or maybe she'd gotten Paul in hot water again.

Maybe he wasn't supposed to be out of the kitchen this close to opening time. Maybe this coffee wasn't free.

Nikki was getting tired of feeling like every move she made was the wrong one. She set her cup on the counter and hurried after Holly. They came face-to-face with a wall of boxes—some of them sagging, some of them with hastily scrawled words on them.

Nikki had never felt so defeated. She wasn't sure how there could even be this much paperwork that hadn't been gone through. Maybe creating delicious recipes took so much energy that there was none left for filing.

"Somewhere in all these boxes are restaurant receipts for the last few years. I need you to dig them out and enter them into my accounting ledger."

"Okay. Uh, any idea where I should start?"

"Not a clue."

"Okay."

Holly walked away, leaving Nikki to stare at the boxes. She was really starting to hate cardboard in a world where she'd always found it quite useful.

After returning to the kitchen, Paul picked up his chef's knife and got to work. The restaurant would open soon. He chopped through the last of the vegetables for the assortment of pastas on the menu that night.

Holly had a pretty decent roasted red pepper pasta,

and as he ran his blade through the veggies, he watched as Nikki walked back and forth from the office to the storage closet, always with something in her hand.

He shouldn't be so interested in her. He had a kitchen to run, and as the first order came in, he was able to focus on his job the way he usually did. "No apps," he called to his line cooks. "Fire one steak and potatoes, medium, one pasta primavera."

He stuck the ticket to the shelf and watched as his cooks sprang into action. The food went into the window minutes later, and Angela returned with another order. Maybe tonight wouldn't be about cleaning and standing around and he'd actually get to cook.

"Fire two steak, one medium, one medium-well, one roasted red pepper pasta, one chicken Florentine." He stepped over to the stove to do the pasta so the other chef could do the chicken. The rush of the busy kitchen, the hiss of meat in a hot pan, and the scent of garlic and onions reminded him of how much he loved his job.

Paul worked quickly, searing the fresh peppers and ladling in the special sauce of roasted peppers, garlic, onion, and cream. The fresh pasta hit the pan last, and Paul tossed everything together with a handful of fresh peas.

"Time on those steaks?" he asked.

"Forty-five seconds, chef."

"Chicken?"

"Ready now, chef."

He plated his pasta, wiping the edges of the bowl and carefully balancing a red pepper rose his prep chef had carved that afternoon in the center. All three plates went in the window, and the waitress whisked them away.

Paul glanced up during a brief interlude between orders to see Nikki coming through with two more boxes.

Angela stepped up to the window to get her order, and she looked at Nikki, too. "Hey, I feel like I haven't seen you all day."

Paul focused on wiping the counter. He wasn't sure how the two knew each other, but it was obvious they were friends.

Nikki looked slightly uncomfortable. Maybe from the heavy boxes. "Holly's kept me pretty busy."

Angela started loading plates into her arms. "Kinda feels like old times working together, right?"

"Uh, not exactly. But at least we're under the same roof." Nikki nodded to the plates in her friend's arms. "Oh, Ang. Five plates?"

Paul almost dove through the opening as Angela startled and nearly dropped all five plates she'd delicately balanced in her arms. "Right." She set two of the plates back in the window. "Whew. Thanks. Makes me really glad you're here."

"Yeah, don't forget it." Nikki sauntered out of the kitchen, almost like she knew Paul was watching and had heard the exchange. And dang, if he didn't like her.

He liked how she'd helped her friend, too, and he appreciated how hardworking Nikki was, trekking back and forth, back and forth with box after box after box. He liked the burgundy sweater she wore, her tight black jeans, and the waves in her auburn hair.

Another order came in, and he swiped it from the board so he would stop fantasizing about a woman he barely knew—who had already insulted him and then thrown coffee on him.

Thankfully, his thoughts stayed schooled through the rest of dinner service. Then he sent his chefs home early, seeing as they'd stayed to clean up without him last night, and put the kitchen back in order by himself.

He paused for a moment, the quietness of the restaurant speaking right to him. He loved cooking, working in a fast-paced environment, and experimenting with food. At Holly Hanson's, he was able to do two of those three things, and he acutely missed trying to match flavor profiles, put in the exact right spice, and find that secret ingredient.

Just like the *cassoulet* needed revamping, Paul needed to create with food. Holly entered the kitchen, but he decided not to say anything to her about it.

"You ready?" She switched off the lights, and he followed her out, wondering when Nikki had left. He stuffed his hands in his pockets and told himself with every step to stop thinking about her.

It didn't work. She plagued him the whole way home and right into his dreams.

Chapter Seven

Nikki blinked, the numbers and lines on the computer screen in front of her blurring together. She blinked again, but the condition only worsened.

Time to go home. She rolled her neck, feeling a sharp, shooting pain in her shoulders and down her back. Yeah, sitting at a desk wasn't any easier than schlepping boxes, and she'd done a lot of both today.

She stood and looked at the clock behind her, shock coursing through her when she saw it was almost one in the morning. She grabbed her phone just to double-check she could still read an analog clock, and sure enough, her phone read 12:53 on the screen.

Leaving Holly's office, Nikki was met by darkness in the kitchen, except for the emergency lights glinting off the stainless steel in ways that seemed abnormal at this hour.

But so was walking through a graveyard at one

a.m. No one did that—by themselves—in the dead of night. "Hello?" she called as she entered the dining room. At least there weren't any sharp objects in here that could mysteriously come to life and stab her.

"Is anyone here?" Her voice echoed around the empty restaurant. She glanced behind her, sure she'd just heard something. No one answered. Nothing moved. "Holly?" Surely, the woman wouldn't have just left her here. Would she?

Of course she would. She probably doesn't even know my name yet!

She approached the front entrance and tried to open it. The handle went down, but the door itself didn't move. She tried the deadbolt, but it just spun.

Her heart leapt to the back of her throat. She was trapped inside this restaurant. At least it wasn't a tiny closet.

"Okay." She heaved a big sigh as she ran through her options. Try to flag someone down? But what would they do? Smash through the front window?

An exasperated laugh bubbled from her throat. But her mouth hadn't gotten her in trouble this time. Just her extreme ability to be forgotten, which wasn't much better. She pulled out her phone and dialed the one person who'd been there for her: Angela.

Please pick up, please pick up. Angela sometimes crashed as soon as she set foot in the apartment, and other times, she nursed a cup of hot chocolate and read a magazine to unwind. Nikki really needed her to have chosen the chocolate tonight. Her chest tightened further with every ring of the phone.

Finally, Angela said, "Hello?"

Relief poured through Nikki like water gushing over a broken dam. "Angela, thank goodness." She inhaled deeply, trying to calm her pulse with pure oxygen.

"Nikki, where are you?"

"I'm...still at the restaurant." She didn't want Angela to think Holly had forced her to stay—or that she'd been forgotten.

"You're putting way too much into this job."

"I didn't mean to. And if you can believe it, I got locked in." She gave a small chuckle, hoping her friend had some sort of ability to get her out of here.

"I'm not even going to ask how," she said in a playful tone. "I wish I could help, but I don't have a key."

Nikki knew who had one. Two people, actually. There was no way on Earth she was calling Holly. But Paul... She wished she'd gotten his number so he could come to her rescue. Maybe then he'd think of her as more than the girl who spilled coffee down his shirt.

Or maybe he'd see her as so inept she got locked inside a building. No, she didn't need another reason to embarrass herself in front of him.

"I think the cleaning crew comes in a few hours," Nikki said. "I'll just leave with them."

"Okay, well, call me if you need anything else."

"Okay."

"Bye."

"Bye." Her voice shook a bit because as soon as she hung up with Angela, she'd be alone again. The call ended, and she lowered her phone. Turning back to the dark restaurant, her stomach growled.

She put one palm over it as a delicious idea occurred to her. She was hungry. She was trapped in a restaurant full of food. And she was a cook.

Excitement filled her as she strode through the restaurant and flipped on the light in the kitchen. Such a glorious sight spread before her. Professional ovens, huge pots to make chili, and more square inches of cooking space than she'd ever been blessed to use. She all but danced into the walk-in refrigerator and collected carrots, onions, and celery. Her eye caught on a beef chuck roast, and she snagged it, an idea for a delectable beef stew coming together in her mind.

She got the stove going, chopped the *mise en place*, and opened a bottle of root beer. Forty-five minutes later, she took the lid off a pot of rice to find perfectly fluffy grains inside. She spooned some onto a plate and ladled the thick beef stew she'd made over it.

Steam rose into the air, bringing with it the scent of braised beef with just a hint of peanut butter. Her mouth watered, and her stomach roared again. She lifted the fork to her mouth and took a bite of beef, carrot, and rice.

Her eyes rolled back in her head, and a sigh passed

through her whole body. Beef stew with root beer. Delicious.

This was where she belonged. Right here, in a kitchen, culinary degree or not. She forked up another bite, the injustice of her situation as frustrating as ever. Maybe she should just go back to school and get her degree. Then she could march right into Finique and wave her resume under that Silent Supervisor's nose.

"What in the world are you doing in my kitchen?" Holly strode forward, her stony-faced mask gone. But the angry version of the celebrity chef was much, much worse.

Being Holly Hanson wasn't easy. No one understood that. Since Henry's visit a couple of days ago, Holly had felt like a yoke had been secured around her neck. She wasn't sure who or what she was tethered to, but that entity never wanted to go in the same direction she did.

Holly knew she didn't want to lose everything she'd worked for years to build, and if she couldn't get her restaurant to bring in more money, Henry would force her to close. She supposed it was his money. And now her new assistant had wasted a bunch of it making something that smelled...scrumptious.

"Oh, my gosh," Nikki said, practically dropping

her fork. "Thank goodness you're here. I—I got locked in."

Holly glanced around, her eyes coming back to Nikki. "Of course I'm here. The alarm company called. The motion detectors went off." She waved to the expensive equipment on the walls.

"Oh, I didn't hear an alarm."

Holly didn't see how that mattered. "Who gave you permission to be in my kitchen?" Nikki probably didn't know how much it cost to buy ingredients, pay to have the lights and electricity work.

She did look sorry about it, and Holly reminded herself that this girl probably meant no harm. "I'm sorry. I just—I was so hungry. I hadn't eaten all day." She looked down at the source of the delicious smell, stuttering in her usual way. Holly really disliked how she could never just say a sentence.

"This cannot happen again."

"No. It won't, ever. I promise. And again, I'm—I'm very sorry."

Holly stared at the dish Nikki had put down. She'd been inspired by simple ingredients such as carrots and beef before. But now? When she looked at a carrot, all she saw was an orange tuber. It was as though her creativity had dried up once the success started.

She advanced slowly, more aware of Nikki's nerves the closer she got. "What exactly is this?"

"Oh, it's just a beef stew I kind of threw together."

Holly drew in a deep breath, getting a salty hint

along with something cloying and suspiciously like sugar. "What is that smell? There's a sweet aroma."

"Oh, I braised the beef in peanut butter and root beer."

Holly jerked her attention back to Nikki, but she was talking with her hands the way she often did and staring at her plate of food like it was a long-lost friend.

But peanut butter and root beer? Such an interesting flavor combination. One that Holly might have thought of in the past, if her mind wasn't so consumed with cookbook deadlines, putting every piece of jewelry in place before she left her apartment, or her bottom line at the restaurant.

"I freestyle when I cook," Nikki continued. "It's sort of my thing. Could I offer you some?" She picked up the plate with the rice and stew, along with a clean fork.

Holly eyed them dubiously, her mind racing. She salivated, hoping the stew tasted as good as it smelled. But she'd had people cook for her before, trying to get credit for an idea Holly might use. Was that what Nikki had done? Maybe she'd just gotten locked in, as she'd said. Holly hadn't cleared the building before leaving. It seemed that her conversations with Henry consumed her thoughts and she forgot little things.

She gave Nikki a look of distrust before scooping some food onto her fork. She turned her head as she put the bite in her mouth, not wanting Nikki to witness her full reaction.

Flavor like she hadn't tasted in years exploded against her tongue. The peanut butter was subtle, barely there in the back of the throat. But the texture of the beef was outstanding—tender and moist—because of the peanut butter.

The sweetness from the root beer was almost a little over the top, but Nikki had tamed it with shallots and garlic and possibly some fish sauce. Holly wasn't quite sure. And she didn't need to be sure right now. The flashing red light she'd indicated earlier had caught everything Nikki had done on camera.

She looked back at the stew, wanting to eat the whole pot. Instead, she asked, "Have you been cooking long?"

Surprise crossed Nikki's expression. "Actually, it's really what I do. Before I came to work for you, I was a cook at Gus's Kitchen downtown. Do you know it? It's a diner."

Holly frowned at the name. Gus's Kitchen. Didn't sound like her kind of place. "I don't do diners."

She cleared her throat and put the plate of stew on the counter. "You know, I really should fire you for this little stunt you pulled."

Nikki shook her head, her eyes wide. "Please don't."

And Holly wasn't going to. She had plans for Nikki—plans that were fluid and moving even as she stood there. But she knew she needed Nikki to stay right here, at the restaurant. "It's not all your fault. I should have made sure you were gone before I locked up."

"So you're not firing me?"

Holly pretended like she was really thinking about it. "No. I was a struggling chef once myself, and I know what a wonderful opportunity it is to get to work in kitchen like this."

"You're going to let me be a cook here?"

Holly half-chuckled and shook her head. "No, of course not."

"Oh." Nikki studied her hands.

Poor girl. Holly really did feel bad for her. And as if someone had snapped their fingers and implanted an idea in her brain, Holly knew what to say to Nikki. "But if you wanted to use the kitchen after hours, I wouldn't object."

Nikki brought back the huge smile she seemed to wear everywhere. Honestly, how she stayed so optimistic all the time was a mystery to Holly.

"You'd really allow that?" she asked.

"As long as we kept it between us. I don't want the rest of my staff to know what a softie I am." Holly had actually never been called such a thing before, but Nikki didn't need to know that.

"Yeah, um, you have my word. I won't tell a soul."

"Great." She glanced over her shoulder to see where the cameras were positioned. All she'd need to do was get in a little early tomorrow and figure out how Nikki had turned beef and carrots into something that tasted like heaven.

"Thank you. Thank you so much! I—Wow." Nikki grabbed onto Holly, startling her and almost knocking her down.

"Ooh." She put her hands on Nikki's shoulders just to keep herself upright and found herself in a hug with the other woman. She hadn't actually embraced another human in a long time, and it felt awkward with this near-stranger. Thankfully, Nikki stepped back quickly.

"I just—it really means a lot to me."

Holly allowed her lips to curl up the slightest bit. At first, she'd found Nikki's idolization of her charming, but now it was just annoying. "Well, why don't you go home? You've had such a long day." She gestured her toward the exit with a light laugh. She moved closer to the stew, her mouth watering at the thought of having another bite—or downing the whole plate. Nikki didn't need to know. No one needed to know.

Nikki looked like she was going to go, but she suddenly turned back. "Oh, by the way, how did you like the stew?"

She gave a half-shrug with her right shoulder. "Oh, it's okay for a novice." She looked straight into Nikki's face, and the woman's expression indicated that the words had hurt. Holly remembered what it was like to search for a hint of approval, and a pin of regret pushed into her heart.

"Great. Thanks." She pressed her lips together, smiled, and finally left.

Holly waited until her footsteps faded, and then she spun back to the stew and picked up the plate. She dug into the food like she hadn't eaten in years. Nikki definitely had some skills in the kitchen, and as the flavors danced on her tongue, Holly smiled, her plan coming together.

"So good."

Nikki was going to help her save her restaurant—what any good assistant would do anyway. She just didn't know it.

Chapter Eight

H olly caught a few hours of sleep after she'd devoured Nikki's beef stew. She woke early to the alarm she'd set and hurried to get ready for the day. Now that she was Holly Hanson, the celebrity chef with cookbooks and TV appearances, she never left the apartment without making sure everything was flawless—from her jewelry to her makeup to her clothes. With her makeup perfect, she took a moment to put a wave in her hair, and she dressed in her navy blue slacks and blazer with a gray silk blouse underneath.

Today, she was going to find out how Nikki had made ordinary ingredients into something so delicious. She was hoping she'd discover a bit of her lost inspiration along the way. If she could just get over to the restaurant before anyone else and figure out how to get the footage off the security tapes, maybe her restaurant could have a future.

She moved through the crypt-like restaurant, her mind spinning. She didn't even like this place that much, but she certainly couldn't let it go now. Not when everything about it kept her at the top of the social circles, allowed her to sign more cookbook deals, and made people turn and stare at her when she walked down the streets of Lakeside.

She paused and turned back to the dining room, allowing herself to accept that she had loved this restaurant once. A long time ago. She remembered opening day, with all the press and cameras. She remembered taking out the first dish to the first customer, a food critic who still stopped by every six months.

But then the restaurant had become work. A job. A chore. Something to be managed, along with dozens of other moving parts of her career. Since she'd left the kitchen to Paul five years ago, Holly found she simply didn't have the same passion for her restaurant. Maybe she just needed to get back in the kitchen. She could get her chef's jacket refitted and get herself back in front of the flattop.

Cooking had quelled her anxiety—the same anxiety now accompanying her steps. She just needed a few new recipes, something to get the wealthy women in this town talking about her again. It didn't matter if one woman no one even knew existed had to be taped to do it.

She rounded the corner into the kitchen and

glanced up to the security camera she'd spotted last night. Still there. Still with a red light beaming down. Turning in a half-circle, she scanned the walls for more cameras, trying to judge which one would give her the best view of the prep area and the stove.

"Hey, Holly."

Holly gasped and spun around to find her executive chef standing there, already dressed in his official clothes. "Paul. What are you doing here?" She looked at her watch. It was barely nine o'clock in the morning, and no one ever came in before noon. "Isn't it a little early to prep for dinner?"

He frowned, probably at the sharp tone of her voice. She couldn't help it. She'd been counting on these few hours before the kitchen staff arrived to do the very secret work she needed to get done.

He studied her. "No. I just wanted to try something out. A recipe I've been working on."

Holly settled her weight on her back foot. This again? "My restaurant, my recipes." She liked Paul because he'd always been able to execute her dishes, and he kept the kitchen clean and humming along, even during the busiest times. Not that there had been many really busy nights lately, not as many as there had been in the beginning of Holly Hanson's days.

"All I ask is for an open mind until you've had a chance to see what I've come up with."

Holly didn't need him to come up with anything, though she was sure Paul could create something great.

Her determination wavered. Maybe she should see if he could pull them from their slump.

No. This is my restaurant. My name on the cookbooks. If he creates the recipes...

She rolled her eyes so he'd know she wasn't happy about this and that she wouldn't like anything he made. "Fine." She could lock her office door and still get her spying done.

"A little early for you to come in, isn't it?" Paul asked.

She swung away from him, not liking the suspicion on his face, and made her voice light. "You know what they say: early bird gets the worm, right?" She walked out, turning back to glare at Paul as she left so he'd know not to question her in the future.

Nikki had done a great job of cleaning up the office, and Holly sat down and fired up the computer. Hopefully, Nikki would be extra-tired after getting locked in. No matter what, she shouldn't be in until noon, which gave Holly a decent amount of time to find the security footage and get some notes taken.

She opened the notebook she'd bought on her way to the restaurant that morning and looked at her desktop, trying to remember where the inspector had told her the security cameras were. Holly had been advised by Henry to have the cameras installed up front so she could discover any problems with her kitchen staff. She'd never been happier to have listened to her investor's advice.

There were four cameras in the kitchen, and it took Holly a couple of tries before she found the right one. The footage came up, and there was Nikki, in full color, depositing an armful of vegetables and the chuck roast on the prep station.

Holly snatched up her pen and started scribbling, keeping the volume of the video footage on silent. Nikki didn't talk to herself as she cooked, but she wore a smile with the size and brightness of the sun and moved with the ease and precision of someone who'd spent a lot of time in the kitchen.

She'd made it almost all the way through the prep of the meal—Nikki had her vegetables sautéing, her meat browning, and the super-distinct braising liquid of peanut butter, root beer, garlic, beef stock, and a dash of Worcestershire sauce—not fish sauce as Holly had suspected—simmering on the stove when Holly's phone rang.

Henry's name showed on the screen, and for the first time in almost six months, Holly didn't send it to voicemail.

Oh no. She wanted to talk to her investor. She swiped the phone on and moved her hand back to pause the video. "Hey, Henry. Thank you for calling me back."

"Yeah, yeah."

She hated his condescending tone, but he'd given her a lot of money for the restaurant, so she always let his comments slide. "Listen, Holly, I've got some bad news. I was able to do some preliminary projections, and your earnings report is worse than I thought."

Bad news? "Meaning?"

"Meaning, you're gonna have to find a way to turn this place around. Or else I can't keep us open much longer."

Holly smiled at the stilled image of Nikki at the stove, a wooden spoon in the pot where the vegetables were softening in butter. "Well, as a matter of fact, I am working on some amazing ideas right now." She hadn't felt this hopeful in a long time, and she hadn't even stepped foot in her kitchen yet.

"I see. Might want to run those by your investor."

Holly's chest squeezed at his disdainful tone, but she let some of her hope and confidence seep into her voice as she said, "I will, I will. As soon as I'm ready. And you will be impressed." Anyone would be wowed by that stew, and Holly knew that recipe was the start of something amazing for her.

"Great. Let me know right away." Henry hung up, and Holly glanced from her phone to the screen, a moment of doubt creeping through her. Then she started the video again and went right back to taking notes. She needed this, and Nikki was an employee at her restaurant.

Paul's creative-chef side had been stewing since the argument with Holly—and Nikki's assessment of the bland *cassoulet*—a few days ago. He'd wanted to do something to revitalize the recipe, but in the end, he'd abandoned the idea.

Fortunately, a new plan had come together that morning. He didn't need to rework one of Holly's tired recipes. He needed to create his own.

The creativity was what had drawn him into the industry in the first place. He'd loved studying flavor pairings in culinary school, learning about savory, sweet, salty, bitter, and earthy combinations and then trying to construct his own recipes that hit on all the right notes.

With Valentine's Day coming up, he was hoping Holly would allow him to add a dish to their usual menu—but after that morning's altercation, some of that positivity had drained away. She had a special way of looking right through him, like anything he said or did would be immediately dismissed.

Still, he weighed flour and mounded it in the middle of his board. After hollowing out a well, he cracked three eggs and added a pinch of salt and a drizzle of olive oil. He loved working with his hands and forming food out of raw ingredients. As he drew more and more flour into the well, the pasta dough came together nicely.

The sound of quick footsteps met his ears, breaking the calm peacefulness that had descended on him as he worked. Nikki came around the corner, her face a ray of sunshine and her smile already in place.

Paul's heart kicked out an extra beat, and his hands stilled in the dough. Nikki was beautiful and so upbeat, bringing a positive vibe wherever she went. Today, she wore a black ribbed sweater with a pair of festive red jeans, along with a silver chain holding a ring.

He glanced away, wondering if the ring was sentimental to her, or if someone special had given it to her.

"Oh, looks like everyone's coming in early today," he said, flashing her a smile of his own. He hadn't flirted in a while, and he wasn't quite sure how to do it.

"Yep. Just trying to make a good impression on Holly." She carried a manila folder, and he wondered what it had inside.

"Maybe you'll last longer than her last few assistants." Paul didn't want to say too much, because Holly was the boss and he felt a sense of loyalty to her for hiring him when he didn't have previous five-star experience. He hoped she and Holly would get along so Holly could focus on the food at her restaurant instead of the receipts. Nikki watched him knead the pasta dough, her smile flipping upside down for a moment.

"Holly can certainly be a challenge to work for," he said.

Nikki sobered the teensiest bit. "Actually, I think she's pretty cool." She grinned again, and the gesture enhanced her beauty enough to distract him momentarily from the food and the conversation.

He nodded and smiled like "cool" was a sufficient adjective for Holly Hanson. "Oh, cool? That's a nice way of describing her."

"You've worked for Holly for a while, haven't you?"

"I have, indeed." He abandoned the dough now, hoping he hadn't already overworked it. He peered at Nikki and decided to up his flirtation game. "How did you know that? Have you been asking about me?" He leaned into the counter to catch a whiff of her perfume over the ingredients sitting between them.

She looked away and down, a sure sign that she had asked about him. Probably Angela, as they'd seemed like old friends.

Nikki exhaled slightly. "Maybe," she said in the flirtiest tone on the planet. She could probably get men to do anything when she spoke in a voice like that.

Paul's stomach flipped. He hadn't actually expected her to admit to her behind-the-scenes espionage.

"Is that so?" He nodded and chuckled, surveying the counter in front of him before returning his gaze to hers. Her eyes sparkled like hazel diamonds, and he wished all this equipment wasn't between them. "Well, what else did you find out?"

Her pink lips puckered and she pretended to think. "Mm. Well, you don't like food critics, you keep a clean and fast-paced kitchen, and you can't stand it when people don't know the difference between a turnip and a parsnip." She started to walk away, as if she'd leave him to his work while she went to get more boxes from the storage closet.

He didn't want her to go, and the super-smile on his face wouldn't fade. "That's some good digging." He wondered who'd told her about the parsnip-turnip thing. He didn't remember saying anything to Angela about that. Had she asked Holly?

Nikki and Holly didn't seem quite to the gossipy-girlfriend stage of their relationship. He couldn't imagine Holly being that close or kind or…vulnerable with anyone. Nikki probably had dozens of girlfriends she shared things with, being as bubbly and warm as she was.

She paused and turned back to him. "Yeah, I mean, aside from being two completely different vegetables, there really isn't much of a difference. Both root vegetables, and both taste pretty much the same." She tacked a cute little giggle onto the end of her critique and left him standing there.

He shook his head, his heart still beating erratically beneath his chef's jacket. She did know specific facts about food, he'd give her that. Some people wouldn't be able to pick a parsnip out of a lineup, let alone know that it was a root vegetable.

While Paul much preferred the flavor of parsnips to turnips—something Nikki couldn't know—she'd pretty much nailed the fact that they were very similar.

She didn't return, and Paul set about making the filling for what he hoped would become a pasta dish on Valentine's Day.

He let the pasta dough rest in the fridge before rolling it through the press and cutting it into large heart shapes. He'd been top of his class at Le Cordon Bleu in sauce-making, and he put together a spicy marinara that would be toned down with the calmer, more subtle flavors of artichokes and mushrooms he planned to put in the filling.

Along with that, he made an Alfredo sauce with parsley to add another texture and a cheesy layer to add richness to an extravagant, romantic dinner.

Plating was not his strongest suit, but he managed to make a sweet potato puree, along with a red pepper hummus. He chilled them until they were firm enough to cut heart shapes he could use on the plates.

He worked methodically, his mind always one step ahead of his hands, always anticipating what the food would taste like. He made sure to take in the smell and sight of the food before he put it in his mouth, and each component was delicious on its own. He was sure it would be a winning dish for Valentine's Day and that Holly wouldn't be rolling her eyes after she tasted it.

Nikki roamed through his mind, taking up the bit of space he had to spare. He should probably do some digging about her, too. Find out if she had a boyfriend, at the very least. But as he put three heart-shaped ravioli on the plate, he realized he didn't even know where to start. He barely knew the woman's last name.

She finally came through the kitchen again, carrying two boxes, and Paul couldn't help himself. He wanted her to stop, talk to him, and give him that brilliant smile she had inside.

"Can I help you with that?"

She slowed to a stop, that smile making an appearance. "Oh. No, thanks. It's helping me with my weight training." She trilled out a laugh that sent fire through him. "I haven't had time to go to the gym. So."

He smiled and looked down at his plates, unsure of what else to say to keep her there.

Her heels clicked a couple of times as she continued to the coffee counter. "Um, mind if I take a peek?" She'd twisted back to him, her face alight with hope.

"Feel free." He waved her over, trying not to show too much enthusiasm.

After setting her boxes next to the carafe, Nikki returned to his station. "Aw, heart-shaped ravioli. Let me guess... For Valentine's Day?"

He waved his hand in the air like a true Italian. "To be determined."

Nikki's eyes edged toward the ceiling as she thought. "And your filling is..." She drew in a deep breath. "Pine nuts..."

He was impressed she could determine that with

just her nose. Maybe she was a chef, too. "With artichoke hearts and mushrooms."

She was nothing but sincere when she said, "Sounds delicious."

"Sounds dreadful." Holly took two steps around the corner, obviously having caught the last part of their conversation. As she made her way over to them, Paul met Nikki's eye. Humiliation deflated his hope, and Paul prepared himself for another argument. He didn't think he could take many more, and for the first time since coming home to Lakeside, he wondered if he should start searching for another job.

He looked down at his rustic ravioli as Holly said, "Rack of lamb, lobster, filet mignon. That's what we serve on Valentine's Day."

Nikki scampered back to her boxes. She clearly didn't think Holly was being cool now, if the scared-animal look in her eye was any indication. A twinge of hurt pressed against Paul's throat at the way she'd left him standing there alone.

"C'mon, Holly, we've been serving those every year on Valentine's Day since I started here. Can't we just switch things up?"

"Not with that." Her disdain for his food couldn't be more obvious. And Nikki had heard and seen it. She stood by her boxes, her hands tucked in her back pockets as she watched, a sympathetic look on her face. Embarrassment heaped on top of his hurt. He didn't need her to have another reason to think he should be replaced.

"Don't you think heart-shaped ravioli is a little amateurish?" Holly's words stung him. He glanced at Nikki, who looked at him with apprehension and that eternal optimism.

He didn't know how to explain Valentine's Day to a woman with no heart. "It's Valentine's Day," he tried anyway, waving his hand like that would make Holly see the holiday was about more than making money. "It's all about hearts and flowers."

"Those are the decorations. Not the cuisine." Her eyes widened as if to say, "Duh, Paul," and she left the kitchen. Left him to face Nikki in all his embarrassment. Her smile had completely disappeared, and he didn't know if she sided with him or Holly. It didn't really matter. She wasn't going to stand up to the celebrity chef on her second day on the job.

And besides, she'd already made her opinion of Holly's executive chef plain. He dropped his gaze to his ravioli—which were delicious and would be a big hit on Valentine's Day if they were given the chance. Nikki mercifully gathered her boxes and left.

Chapter Nine

Nikki dug through box after box of paper. She regretted wearing the long-sleeved sweater, though it probably had saved her from half a dozen cardboard cuts. She'd been able to locate probably a month's worth of receipts, and with every passing hour, she felt like she was falling further and further behind.

After Holly had humiliated Paul in the kitchen, Nikki had avoided him, even going out to the sandwich shop down the street to grab something to eat. He probably didn't want her sympathy, and besides, she couldn't think of anything to say—a first for her. His kindness when she'd insulted him stuck in her brain, and she figured the nicest thing to do for him was to give him some space.

She'd thought his ravioli were beautiful, and she'd wanted to try one. Well, what she'd really wanted was for him to feed her one, maybe while they were on their own romantic date.

She worked at a feverish pace, mostly to get her mind to stop conjuring up fantasies about the handsome chef around the corner from the closet where she sifted through slips of paper with barely legible print on them.

Holly shouldn't have cut him down so quickly. Nikki couldn't get the tortured look on his face out of her mind. He'd seemed genuinely embarrassed that she'd witnessed the whole thing.

I should've given them more privacy, she thought for the tenth time. She'd really enjoyed flirting with Paul. The spark between them seemed instant, and she didn't want him to feel uncomfortable around her.

Finally, when the restaurant was about to close, she moved through the kitchen, noticing a difference in the way Paul interacted with the cooks, but she couldn't put her finger on what exactly had changed. She needed to find Angela, and she did, as her friend was just finishing up with her last table.

"Hey, Ang," Nikki called.

"Yeah?" Her friend came closer, and Nikki contemplated asking her a little bit more about Paul. The first two things Nikki had listed earlier were obvious stuff she'd learned simply by observing him. But the parsnip had come from Angela—well, Jerrod really, as Nikki had asked Ang while she was flirting with Jerrod.

"Listen, I'm going to be working late tonight, so don't wait up for me." She carried some floppy folders she hoped would have a few receipts she needed. Her feet hurt, but she was getting used to the aches and pains of working long days in heels.

"Yeah, I'm staying late, too," Angela said.

"Really?"

"Yeah, it's Sunday night."

Nikki searched her face, waiting for more.

"Paul cooks dinner for the staff. It's, uh, kind of a ritual." The way Angela smiled and seemed happy to stay late on a Sunday night made Nikki long for that kind of close friendship with a group of people. She had Angela, and well, that was about it now that Gus's had closed.

"That sounds fun." Nikki wondered what it would take to get an invitation. Everyone at Holly's seemed nice, and a little more time with Paul couldn't hurt. Maybe in a group, she wouldn't feel like she needed to avoid him.

"It is. You should join us."

She half-laughed as she turned away. "Maybe I will," she said in a coy voice, hoping Angela didn't see right through her to her reasons for wanting to stay and eat.

And it wasn't because she was hungry.

As she stepped back into the kitchen, she realized why the atmosphere was different. Paul wasn't the boss anymore. He was just a man, talking to his friends as they put together dinner for their other friends.

Twenty minutes later, she heard him say, "Dinner's on," and she left Holly's office to join the rest of the staff. Thankfully, Angela had saved her a seat with her and Jerrod, and the chefs began bringing out salad and a scrumptious-smelling pappardelle.

Nikki ate with gusto, her last meal being hours ago. Paul was busy with the staff, laughing and talking like he was just one of the guys. She kept tabs on him, noticing when he was near and missing him when he ran back to the kitchen for more bread or to bring someone extra Alfredo sauce.

Her crush seemed huge, and she felt a bit ridiculous. She'd only known him for a few days—but she liked him—and she wanted more time to learn more about him.

He finally made his way to their table and flipped a chair backward before he sat down. He wore a blue sweater that made his biceps and arms look bigger than they did in the chef's jacket.

"So? What does our resident food critic have to say?"

She laughed and rolled her eyes, tucking her hand on the back of her neck for some reason. Was that considered flirting?

No matter what, she enjoyed his presence, his attention, and his wonderful smile.

"Is the pappardelle up to your standards?"

"You're never going to drop that, are you?" She wasn't sure she wanted him to, and her flirtatious tone said as much.

"Eventually." He nodded toward her nearly empty plate. "So, how is it?"

"It's really good." Her voice sounded fake even to her, and the way her head bobbled like those dolls... No way he believed her.

His blue eyes studied her, and she thought the little squint he did was simply adorable. "I sense a *but*," he said.

"What? No! No, not at all."

"Okay. Come on, give me your review." He waggled his fingers like he was calling someone toward him.

She really didn't want to hurt his feelings, and the pappardelle was really delicious. She sensed, though, that he wasn't going to let this go.

"Well, I'm no food critic," she said.

"We've already established that."

She shook her head and giggled. Maybe she should just tell him it was the best pappardelle she'd ever eaten, because it was.

Paul sobered and said, "Please. You can be honest with me."

A moment passed between them, and their eyes locked together. He wasn't smiling and neither was she, and this felt like the first real moment they'd shared.

She exhaled, hoping she wasn't about to ruin her chance with the only man who'd interested her in a solid year.

"Okay, the only thing I noticed, and—and seriously, it's excellent—but, it's just that I've tasted this exact same pappardelle at other restaurants. I mean, yours is, by far, one of the best I've ever had." He nodded, seeming to absorb what she was saying. "But...there's nothing about it that tells me that you made it."

His eyebrows shot up on her last words, like she'd spiked something into his chest, and her heart bumped out an extra beat. "Oh, I'm sorry, Paul. I didn't mean to offend you. It's just, I can be a little opinionated when it comes to food. I just—" She sighed. He wouldn't look away from her, his beautiful eyes practically begging her to explain things right. "I guess I just have my own style of cooking."

"Your own style of cooking?"

Nikki didn't know how to explain it, and still, he waited for more. The best thing to do would be to show him, and Holly had given her permission to use the kitchen and the restaurant's ingredients after hours...

"Yeah." She stood and reached for his hand. "Come on, I'll show you."

Paul wasn't sure if he was watching Nikki cook or perform a comedy act. She'd pulled out the most random ingredients, set a pan on the stove, and gotten to work.

Yogurt, honey, potatoes. None of it really went together. But things had turned really weird when she'd gotten out the ice cream cones.

Now she had her chicken sizzling in the pan, the potatoes out of the oven, and she seemed like she might be open to conversation. She hadn't told him expressly that she didn't like to talk while she cooked, but he'd gotten the message after he'd tried to ask her a couple of questions early on.

She moved with ease in the kitchen, held knives and utensils like she'd used them all before, and once again, Paul wished he had someone to ask about her past. She'd definitely worked as a cook, and he really wanted her to work with him.

"Almost done," she said, and he took that as an invitation to speak.

He grinned and picked up one of the leftover ice cream cones. "Ice cream cones. I can see it in a dessert, but in a dinner recipe?"

"I dredged the bird in yogurt and honey, then coated it in the cones and onto the fryer." She waved her tongs and acted like he hadn't been here to watch the whole thing. She moved over to the frying pan, which had been through a couple rounds of chicken. She'd made sure to add more oil and bring the pan back to high heat before adding the new pieces, almost like a pro.

She picked up the pan and came back to him. "It's like chicken and waffles, all in one." She was as giddy as a five-year-old on Christmas, and her excitement was palpable and definitely infectious.

Paul leaned into the counter with both hands. "That sounds just perfect—for a county fair." He grinned and flashed her a smile.

Nikki, in all her flirtatious glory, wagged the tongs at him. "You're a real food snob, you know that?"

He wanted to taste her chicken, which did smell divine...and her lips. Instead, he raised his hands and said, "I studied at Le Cordon Bleu."

She gave him a look of resignation and set down her chicken pan. "Of course you did."

He chuckled, enjoying this exchange with her more than he'd enjoyed anything in a long, long time. "What is that supposed to mean?"

Her brilliant smile returned. "It's just..." She giggled, everything about her lighting up a dark part of Paul he'd sort of forgotten about. "Well, you know. Schools like that are very structured. Very black and white. There's not a lot of room for gray."

"But those are the tools that a chef needs in order to rise above the mediocre." He knew now that she wasn't a trained chef. A very good cook, yes. But a chef, no. "To me, gourmet cooking is a fine art."

She seemed to hear him, and some of his words may have even let some air out of her enthusiasm. "Yeah, well, what about abstract art? Hmm?" She kept her eyes on her plate as she arranged the chicken with the potatoes.

He chuckled. "I'm guessing that's your preference."

She looked at him with those big, beautiful eyes. "I'm just saying, crayons can make art, too."

Smart and beautiful, a dangerous combination. "Fair enough." He clapped his hands together and fell back half a step.

Nikki pushed the plate closer to him. "Okay." She placed her hands in a praying gesture under her chin and watched as he selected a piece of chicken and brought it to his mouth.

He took a bite, the crunch from the waffle cones absolutely providing excellent texture to the moist chicken underneath. He tasted the sweetness of the honey, the tang from the yogurt, and somehow, she'd balanced it all with just the right amount of salt.

Paul frowned at the chicken, wondering how three sweet things had turned out not sweet at all. He glanced at her and found her face filled with hope and anxiety.

"So?"

He put the chicken down and stepped around the corner of the counter, which he'd been using as a barrier between them. He couldn't seem to look at her, probably because he'd lunge forward and try to kiss her, and he didn't think that would be appropriate.

"It's apparent you're not a cook."

She deflated completely, her hands falling to her sides as she faced the counter where her chicken sat.

"You are a chef. This is outstanding."

She yanked her gaze back to his, and her beauty struck him full in the chest. "Do you really mean that?" She grinned, and he wanted her to smile at him like that every day.

"You certainly have a style."

She giggled. "Thanks. You have no idea what it means to me to hear you say that. I mean, I love this job, but I just miss being in the kitchen. So."

He loved the way she added "so" to the end of a lot of her sentences, loved the way the lights shone on her reddish-brown hair, loved that she was so humble that she didn't even know she'd just created the best fried chicken he'd ever tasted.

Picking up a piece of chicken, he passed it to her. "Cheers to you, food critic Nikki Turner." He chose a drumstick as she looked at him with stars in her eyes.

"We're cheers-ing chicken?"

"What else would you expect from an uptight, structured, Cordon Bleu, executive chef?"

She laughed, but he simply brought the chicken back to his mouth, because it was that good.

Chapter ten

Nikki had forgotten what doing nothing felt like. It seemed impossible that just a couple of weeks ago, she'd done whatever she wanted all day long. She loved her job, but the late nights in the kitchen, concocting her recipes and exercising her culinary muscles, left her more exhausted than she'd predicted.

She ran down to Delucci's and grabbed some of the biscotti and cinnamon rolls she'd become so fond of. Even days off needed carbs. She laid some breakfast treats out on a plate just as Angela sat at the bar. "Oh, it's so nice to be here and just relax today." Nikki gave Angela a smile. Their days off had never matched up so well, but neither of them had to go in today.

"You must be exhausted," Angela said. "You've had a lot of late nights this week. I hope Holly is paying you overtime." She raised her eyebrows, and a slice of guilt cut through Nikki.

"She is. Sort of." She spun around to the coffeemaker

so Angela wouldn't be able to see the hint of a lie in her eyes. After all, Nikki couldn't tell Ang the reason she didn't get home until one-thirty in the morning was because she was busy making clam and corn chowder with bacon or mac and cheese with broccolini and sausage. And last night, she'd taken beef smoked sausage and paired it with grits made with parmesan and asiago cheeses. The sweet-salty combination had been a dance against her taste buds, and Nikki smiled as she turned back to Angela.

"You deserve a medal for putting up with her."

She busied herself with the sugar and cream for the coffee. "No, she's seriously not that bad. She's been pretty nice to me."

"Okay, I can't quite wrap my head around that, but..." She shrugged one shoulder. "Maybe you remind her of herself when she was young."

She poured the coffee into the mugs. "Hmm, maybe." Nikki wondered if that really was the case. Holly had mentioned that someone had given her a break early in her career, and Nikki hoped a recipe she tried in the professional kitchen at Holly's would lead her to somewhere similar.

Angela sipped her coffee. "By the way, I picked up a shift on Valentine's Day."

Nikki stared at her, a thread of desperation pulling through her. "You mean I have to watch *When Harry Met Sally* all by myself this year?"

Ang had the decency to look sympathetic. "Well,

as much as I want to reminisce about the cons of Valentine's Day and eat chocolate, it's a big night for tips." Nikki had to admit her logic made sense. Angela needed all the tips she could get, and Nikki couldn't be upset about that.

But it would be hard to be home alone. Though two years had passed since Ryan's disastrous breakup with her, Nikki still felt like she needed some extra support.

A smile brightened Angela's face. "Not to mention, this way I can say I spent Valentine's Day with Jerrod."

"Okay." She handed Angela a teal oversized mug—her friend's favorite. Nikki had given it to her the first Christmas they'd lived together in Lakeside. She lifted her green mug with the purple and red flowers. "Hey, how do you like working with Paul?"

A knowing look came across Angela's face. "Paul? As in executive chef Paul?" She grinned like Nikki had just cracked the funniest joke on the planet.

"Yeah, Paul, as in the-guy-who's-cooking-behind-the-stove-all-day Paul." She hoped Angela wouldn't make a big deal out of the question. She'd asked about him before, but Jerrod had taken over and given all the information. Now that Nikki thought about it, Angela hadn't contributed much about Paul but had spent most of the time watching Jerrod with a dreamy smile on her face.

Angela ducked her head. "Don't tell me you're crushing on him."

"What? No!" She lowered her mug as Angela raised her eyebrows in a silent, *Really?*

"Come on," Nikki said. "I just think he's a really talented chef. Besides, I don't crush on people. It's not my thing."

"Oh no, of course not."

Okay, maybe she had been crushing a little, but she didn't think she'd been too obvious about it. She'd enjoyed their conversations, and cooking for him had been as terrifying as it had been exhilarating. He'd liked her food. Called her a chef.

All right, she was totally crushing on him.

"So," Angela said. "But you guys have been chatting, right?"

"Yeah, we've had a few conversations here and there. Nothing big." As she spoke, Nikki realized that most of their flirting and talking had happened in five-minute increments while he prepped or she carried a box through the kitchen. She'd like more than that, but Holly's rule about employees dating struck her mind like lightning. Paul was handsome and talented, and Nikki needed more time to get to know him better before she could decide if she wanted to break one of Holly's rules.

"Really. So what have you guys been chatting about?" She lifted one shoulder in a shrug, clearly disbelieving everything Nikki said.

"Cooking and recipes and stuff."

"Huh. Yeah, sounds boring. Although, for a couple

of chefs, sounds like you two might have a lot in common." She gave Nikki a knowing grin.

"Okay, you're reading way too much into this." Maybe Nikki had, too. They had only talked about superficial things, exchanged some banter about how potatoes were the perfect food for any meal, day or night, and whether or not he should add nutmeg to his ravioli filling for that secret something. She didn't know anything about his family or his childhood, nothing.

"Am I?" Angela lifted her mug to her lips, and Nikki scoffed her slight frustration out with a laugh.

She couldn't deny it, though—she was interested in getting to know Paul. A quick thought stole through her mind. Maybe he would have to work on Valentine's Day, too, and maybe Nikki should go in so she could say she spent it with him...

Paul bounced the basketball, glad for a day off. He took them rarely, but since Holly had humiliated him about the ravioli, and Nikki had said his food had no personality, he'd needed an afternoon to himself to figure things out.

He'd been working at Holly Hanson's for five years. Cooking her recipes. Sending out her food. He felt like he'd lost a bit of himself, and from Nikki's critique, it sounded like it was showing in his food.

He wasn't upset with her—quite the opposite. He couldn't see that his style had become stale, and he appreciated her fresh eyes and seasoned taste buds. Plus, he'd sure enjoyed watching her cook in his kitchen, and that wouldn't have happened without her honesty about his pappardelle.

He'd wanted to be alone for a couple of hours, but he was glad he wasn't flying solo now. He'd never worried too much about not having friends, but he had to admit it was nice to be able to text Jerrod and get together with him. This morning, though, Jerrod had called Paul, wanting to know if Paul could meet him at the recreational center basketball court. Paul had known what that meant—girl troubles.

Sure enough, Jerrod had been talking non-stop about Angela for an hour. Paul didn't mind. He even thought briefly about asking Jerrod about Nikki. He didn't think the poor guy could focus on anything but his own dilemma, though.

Jerrod reached in and swiped the ball from Paul, who was distracted by thoughts of how to give dating advice.

"If you're smart about it, Holly will never find out," Paul said.

Jerrod cocked his head in surprise. "Angela's best friend is Nikki, and Nikki is Holly's assistant." He shot over Paul's head. The ball went straight in, as it usually did.

Paul grabbed the rebound and went to the top of

the key, palming the ball as he thought about Nikki. "I wouldn't worry about it. I don't think that Nikki would say anything to Holly."

"You don't know that for sure."

"I've got a feeling about her," he said, hoping he wasn't giving away too much. He didn't really have a relationship with Nikki, but the possibility of one kept his mouth shut for the time being. "I just don't think that she would."

Jerrod looked tormented. "Because if I wait too long to ask her out, then I run the risk of her meeting someone else." He was right back to Angela. No acknowledgment that maybe Paul was right, that his feelings about Nikki—whatever those were—could be spot-on. Paul could probably tell Jerrod he'd proposed to Nikki, and Jerrod would wonder if Angela would even go out with him if he asked.

"That is true." He threw the ball to Jerrod, nearly done with their one-on-one game.

"And if I ask her out now, I run the risk of getting fired." He tossed the ball back.

"Tough choices, my friend. Tough choices." Paul grinned at Jerrod, faked left, and went right, going in for the easy lay-up. They played for a while longer, and Jerrod left without a firm commitment to getting a date with Angela.

Paul understood Jerrod's hesitation. A job at Holly Hanson's didn't come easy, and Jerrod had been bartending there for a few years now. It was hard to give up something great, even if he could possibly get something greater.

He might lose his job only to break up with Angela in three months, or six, or a year. Paul wasn't normally so negative, but he understood that Jerrod had a lot to consider before asking Angela for a date.

His thoughts wandered again to Nikki. He hadn't been out with anyone in a long time—since opening the restaurant with Holly, in fact. A frown crossed his face.

Maybe he should be committing to asking someone out. Get out of the kitchen every once in a while, expand his horizons.

He hadn't thought like this in years, and he knew what the catalyst was—or rather, *who* the catalyst was.

Nikki.

She'd obviously cooked in a professional kitchen before, and he wanted to know which one. He needed to just man up and ask her about more than why she put ice cream cones on chicken.

She'd definitely seemed interested in him, so he shouldn't be too afraid to simply talk to her. Maybe Holly's rule about employees dating had gotten under his skin, too. But Nikki seemed nice, and he sensed a gentle soul in her he wanted to know better.

After he left the gym, he wandered to Lakeside's downtown farmers' market, where vendors displayed homemade trinkets, antiques, and a plethora of fruits, flowers, and vegetables from the more temperate coast several miles away.

Paul browsed a selection of heirloom tomatoes before moving on to a selection of apples out of Washington. One of his favorite childhood memories came with the crisp, sweet scent of apples as his grandmother taught him how to make a *torta di mele*—an apple tart with custard and cinnamon bread. He could practically smell the cinnamon and apples baking, and the way the bread had soaked up all the eggy custard made his mouth water right there on the street.

He'd just picked up an apple when he caught a glimpse of Nikki's reddish-brown hair. Sure enough, she wove through the customers in the stand, her arms laden with bags of produce.

As far as he knew, she only lived with Angela, and Holly didn't buy produce for the restaurant from the farmers' market. So what was Nikki doing with all of those fruits and vegetables?

He put down the golden delicious apple that he knew made the best *torta di mele* and ducked out of the farmers' market to follow Nikki.

She wore a pink coat, so she was easy to spot, even through all the downtown pedestrian traffic. Paul wasn't sure why he didn't just catch up with her and find out what was going on. Something told him to hang back, watch, and see where she went.

He listened to that voice as she walked several

blocks with her heavy bags. Eventually, she entered the community center, and he was sure he would lose her. The center sponsored so many programs it would be impossible to know where she'd gone if he didn't see which way she went inside the building.

Hurrying past the main doors, he peered in the window, trying to catch a glimpse of her. His pulse bobbed in the back of his throat for some reason, like he was a Peeping Paul and would get caught any moment, hauled down to the police station, and questioned about why he was so interested in this woman.

He wouldn't be able to answer, he knew that. There was simply something intriguing about her that called to him.

He felt very much like a cat burglar as he sidled up to the window, his back more to it than his chest, and peered over his shoulder through the dirty glass. He didn't see her, and his heart sank down to his toes.

He'd lost her. He sank against the brick building for a few moments, trying to figure out if he should go inside and try to track her down or forget about this slightly stalker-ish moment in his life.

He twisted, and there she was. His breath caught as he took in the curve of her body without the coat. She wore a blue and white flowered shirt, and she finished tying a white apron around her waist.

She moved down a table laden with vegetables and began unwrapping a giant head of romaine lettuce. Glancing up, she looked directly at him.

He froze. She did, too.

Then that wonderful, warm smile spread her lips, and Paul's heart thundered for a couple of reasons. One, he'd been caught, and two, her eyes didn't seem to be able to unlock from his.

She waved as if to say, *Are you gonna stand out there and stare? Or come in?*

Something sparked in Paul's blood, and he knew he only had one choice. He was going in. He waved back, feeling foolish at the same time hope bloomed in his chest. She'd gestured for him to come in, and he couldn't deny her.

They both chuckled as they walked toward each other. Paul removed his gloves and drank in the scent of her perfume and the way she carried herself with grace and confidence.

"Are you spying on me?"

"No. I was…following you." He laughed, enjoying the way she made him feel, though he couldn't even categorize what the emotion was.

She giggled and tucked her hair. "Oh-kay."

He should just come clean so she didn't think he was a creepy stalker. "I saw you at the farmers' market and I was wondering…what's with all the produce?"

"Well, now you know."

"So you work here?"

"No, no, I just volunteer here. The center serves free meals to families—or anyone, really, who's in need or hungry, so I cook here twice a week."

Paul pointed over her shoulder. "What's on today's menu?" He hoped he could stay, spend time with her, be where she was.

She turned back to the prep station and said, "There's red lentil soup with bacon and turnips. Then we have ham, chicken, and cheese sandwiches. The ham and cheese are left over from last night." She reached for a piece of ham and layered it on a slice of bread.

Everything about this place spoke to him. No, it wasn't gourmet food—not even close—but it was good food for good people. "I'm beginning to understand where you developed your style."

"Oh, I see. My style is too refined for you?"

"Pass me a knife; I'll start chopping."

She looked at him with an edge of interest and desire in her eyes he hadn't seen before. Sure, at the restaurant, they'd talked, maybe even flirted with the way they'd clinked chicken drumsticks before eating them several nights ago.

But this look was something different. This look indicated that she was interested in getting to know him better, too.

And so he chopped, washed lettuce, and did whatever else Nikki set him to do. The panini presses came out, and sandwiches went on as volunteers worked to get lunch ready to serve.

Paul watched as Nikki stood in front of a large pot of soup and tasted it. Her face said it was definitely lacking something, and she sprinkled a spice into it, then smiled in a self-satisfied way.

"Cardamom? In that?"

"Mm-hm." Nikki picked up a clean spoon, dipped it in the broth, and extended her arm for him to try the soup. It could've been a romantic moment between them if not for all the volunteers.

Paul schooled his thoughts and focused on the spicy, almost citrusy taste the cardamom gave to the soup. "You're right." He nodded, more than happy to be wrong in this instance. "Gives it the kick."

She grinned. "It's that abstract crayon I was talking about."

Paul was starting to understand what she meant. Just because the red lentil soup came from an oversized pot on a single burner didn't mean it wasn't absolutely beautiful food.

He gazed at her as she continued working and thought of how she didn't seem to fit in anywhere, either, yet she was gorgeous and brilliant wherever she went.

Chapter Eleven

Nikki couldn't shake Paul's gaze. Not that she cared too much. He seemed to be watching her extra close, almost like he wanted to take notes of what she was doing. She didn't mind that he questioned her use of spices because she really enjoyed having him work with her.

Besides, the center could always use more help, and when would they ever get a Cordon-Bleu-trained chef again?

Probably never, Nikki thought with a note of sadness. Though Paul seemed to enjoy his time at the community center, he worked too much to make it a regular habit.

After lunch ended and everything had been cleaned up—Paul stayed to help through all of that, too—Nikki shrugged into her coat and found him waiting by the front door.

Waiting for her, she hoped, and when he turned

and his whole face lit up at the sight of her, she couldn't help but return the smile.

"Should we walk?" he asked.

She tucked her hair behind her ear and nodded, glad to go with him and perhaps spend an evening with him that didn't involve chef jackets, recipe talk, or the threat of Holly interrupting them.

"I hope we didn't work you too hard today."

"No, it was fun. I really enjoyed it. A nice change from working for Holly."

"Yeah?" Nikki glanced into the sky, thinking it was going to rain later. "Why do you stay there?" she asked, hoping it wasn't too personal. She also realized her voice had come out a bit on the accusatory side, so she added, "I mean, just because you could work anywhere."

He spread his arms wide for a moment, as if trying to gather the world into the palms of his hands. "Holly gave me my start. I owe her."

"Mm." She could see that. Paul was a loyal guy. But it seemed like his loyalty might be better served somewhere else. "I guess the food's just not as I imagined, you know? I thought it'd be more... innovative."

"You know, Holly's problem is that she tries to control everything." He stepped slightly in front of her on the sidewalk and stopped walking. Nikki appreciated this little insight into Holly, who had treated her nicely for the most part when it seemed like everyone else got a different version of the woman. Maybe she should be more wary of Holly.

"She wasn't always like that," Paul continued. "The Holly that gave me my start was original, collaborative. She's changed."

Nikki heard the underlying tone of sadness in Paul's voice, and she tried to give him a reassuring look. It was an epic failure, so she dropped her gaze to the sidewalk and let it wander up the building behind him. A sign in the window caught her attention.

"A pop-up shop?" She nodded so he'd look, too. The green and pink sign read, "One day only! Dessert shop."

Paul looked at it and back to her. "Yeah. Yeah, it's this really cool idea. You can rent unused spaces for a couple of days, and pop-up your own shop, so to speak."

Nikki loved the idea, and it started swirling around in her head. "Nice."

He pointed toward the pop-up dessert shop. "Hot chocolate?"

"Yeah, sure." Not only did Nikki want to see what this pop-up shop business was all about, but the afternoon had started to cool into evening, and hot chocolate would be a welcome addition to her life. If he paid for her drink, was this a date?

If he didn't... Well, Nikki wouldn't know what to make of that. Thankfully, he didn't force her brain to derail because he paid for both of their hot chocolates and handed her one.

She liked the abundance of laugh lines around his eyes when he smiled. It made him look truly happy, and she basked in that joyful glow as they made their way back out onto the street.

The breeze tugged at her hair as they left behind the taller buildings of downtown and moved into Liberty Park, which boasted of a large pond with miles of walking paths surrounding it.

He asked where she'd cooked before, and she started talking about the first restaurant—Alfredo & Sons—where she'd learned how a busy kitchen functioned. Maybe not as busy as his, and nowhere near as fancy, but Nikki felt content talking about her early days in front of the stove.

When she realized she'd babbled about herself through half of her hot chocolate, she asked him about his family and learned he was an only child and had grown up right here in Lakeside. He didn't speak much about that before he moved on to his days in Paris.

Nikki liked being with him, enjoyed the sound of his voice, and even thought once or twice about brushing her gloved hand against his just to see what he would do. She decided to keep her hands to herself so as to not be so obvious.

"Where else did you cook?" he asked.

"Most recently, I was at Gus's Kitchen." Wistfulness

wound through her, and she wished she had a bowl of her spicy, cinnamon candy chili right now.

"You cooked at Gus's Kitchen? Loved that place."

She looked at him to see if he was being serious. He seemed to be. "Really? I never would've figured you as a diner guy." She giggled, the sound floating across the water.

"Just because I cook gourmet cuisine doesn't mean that's all I eat."

She nodded, enjoying the playfulness between them. "Okay."

The scenery around her was gorgeous with its expansive lawns. Though they were mostly brown right now, she imagined them in their summer glory. The trees would also be beautiful once all the leaves came back this spring. Nikki loved this park in the summer and in the winter, even as skeletal as the tree branches were.

"So what happened at Gus's?" Paul asked. "I never heard why it closed."

"Oh, it's sad, really. He tried really hard to sell the place, but everyone wants a modern restaurant these days. No one wants a diner." She shook her head to rid herself of the melancholy feeling, but it wouldn't go. "So, anyway, he decided to retire, and his kids didn't want to take it over."

"I've had a few of those discussions myself."

She looked up at him, and his blue eyes held a bit of regret.

"My dad wanted me to take over the family business," he explained. "I had other plans."

"Oh, the age-old tale of father-son disagreement." They continued around the pond and took a boardwalk out to a lookout.

"What about you?" he asked.

"Well, uh, my mom was a waitress, and my dad is a restaurant food supplier. So I guess, in a way, I did go into the family business."

The quacking of ducks and the setting sun added to their conversation, and though Nikki had been on the go all day, there was nowhere she'd have rather been. She sipped her hot chocolate and snuck a peek at Paul. Perfectly handsome, talented, sensitive Paul.

She was glad she'd gotten to know a little bit more about him today, not all of it coming through conversation. She hoped there would be future days like this one. Maybe even one with hearts and flowers, which was coming up very soon.

Paul strolled along with Nikki at his side. The day had turned out to be exactly what he'd needed, though nothing he'd done had been on his radar when he'd woken up that morning. His conversation with Jerrod wouldn't leave his mind, because he found himself flirting with the idea of disobeying Holly and actually asking Nikki out on a date.

The sun reflected off the pond, and he pulled in a breath at the beauty of it. He glanced at Nikki, who was likewise as radiant. "Is this the best hot chocolate or what?"

"It is really good. Except there's some ingredient in it I just can't put my finger on."

"Lavender."

"Mm. Of course. So good." They reached the end of the boardwalk and stood with the pond surrounding them on three sides. She leaned against the railing and gazed up at him with those honey-hazel eyes. "You know, the only thing that would make this better would be an almond biscotto from Delucci's. Do you know that place?"

Paul seized, searching her face for any hint of comedy. When he didn't find any, he asked, "Is that a joke?"

She seemed perplexed as she wiped her fingertips across her forehead. "No. Just a question."

He stared at her, trying to figure out what was going on.

"Why are you looking at me like that?" she asked.

"My last name is Delucci." It wasn't exactly a secret, and he wasn't sure why he'd chosen this moment to be self-conscious about who he was and where he'd come from. He tried to laugh, but it didn't really come out right.

Understanding crossed through her eyes. "Marty and Trish are your parents?"

"Wait. You know them?" And by their first names, too. Paul wasn't sure if he should be horrified or grateful. He wondered what they'd said about him—if they'd even spoken of him.

"Are you kidding?" Her trademark grin burst onto her face. So they hadn't said anything negative. He should be grateful for that.

"I've gone in there like every day for the last two years," she continued. "Although, I've gone in there less since I started working for Holly, but…it's funny. When I told them I started working there, they…they didn't mention you." She seemed to really be searching her memories, too, but Paul was glad she didn't have any.

"Makes sense. It's no secret that my father and I don't have the best relationship." He once again tried to laugh to mask the pain in his voice, the same pain that radiated throughout his body, but only a breathy sound came out.

He didn't need to relive those arguments, didn't want to recall the anger and abandonment on his father's face, didn't want to remember how he'd left for Paris in the middle of the night without anyone to say goodbye to.

"Delucci's is the family business you didn't go into," she said.

"Yup." He smiled tightly and looked out over the water. "I wanted to go to Paris, study at Le Cordon Bleu. My father saw that as a slap in the face. He couldn't understand why I would want something different than him and my grandfather. We both stood our ground with my mom in the middle. Long story short, we don't see much of each other these days." He looked back to Nikki, hoping for and finding sympathy.

Truth was, while Paul didn't want to bake biscotti and knead bread for a living, he did love his parents. They didn't have any other children, and his father had planned to pass the bakery to Paul.

He had no idea what his dad would do with Delucci's Bakery once he was ready to retire. Selling it would be really hard for Paul to watch. He couldn't imagine what it would be like for his father, who had dedicated his life to the shop.

The guilt he'd felt over that had spurred him to give baking a try. And while he hadn't hated his time with his hands in dough, he'd known it wasn't what he was meant to do. There'd been arguments, then silence.

Paul hadn't kept going back for more, and his father hadn't tried to fix the rift between them, either. Not being able to have his parents fully in his life was hard. Maybe harder than he'd ever realized before. Suddenly, the fact that he didn't have anyone to confide in slapped him right in the face. Who would he tell if Holly let him put the heart-shaped ravioli on the menu? Who would he tell if he created the most amazing recipe? Or opened his own restaurant?

His father didn't want to hear it, and his mother couldn't bear to play the middleman. Paul had friends at work, but he didn't have anyone to truly share his life with. He had never felt as lonely as he did in that moment, looking at Nikki, as they stood on the boardwalk with dozens of ducks surrounding them.

"I'm sorry," she said. "I wish there was something I could do to help."

He shook his head and shrugged. "It's okay. It is what it is." He put on a smile. "But you are right. One of their biscotti would go great with this right now."

This time, when he laughed, it actually sounded like a laugh. And when Nikki joined hers to his, he thought maybe she could be the one he could share his life with.

Chapter twelve

Nikki woke the next morning, snug and warm in her bed, a smile already on her face. Because Paul was on her mind and had starred in most of her dreams. She was glad he'd followed her from the farmers' market the previous morning, even if it had been a little strange. They'd spent the rest of the day together, and she'd learned a lot about him.

While the hot chocolate had been delicious, the real treat had been him. She grinned as she got ready and left her apartment. Her steps slowed and her enthusiasm to get to the restaurant waned as she approached Delucci's Bakery.

She paused at the corner and glanced in the window. Should she say anything? Just get her coffee and go?

Neither Trish nor Marty seemed to be at the counter, and only a few people lingered at the tables, picking off pieces of their *panettone* or *zeppole*. Her mouth watered at the thought of Italian fruitcake or doughnuts, but she'd probably stick with her biscotti. Or maybe she'd indulge and get a jelly-filled doughnut—a *bomboloni*, if she wanted to try speaking Italian.

In the end, she slipped into the bakery and approached the counter. Trish spotted her and came over, sending Nikki's heart jumping.

"Morning, Trish. I'm just gonna have a black coffee today." No doughnuts, no biscotti, no latte. Nikki hardly recognized herself.

"You got it." Trish moved away to fill the to-go cup, returning only a moment later.

Nikki considered just picking up her cup and going. But Trish and Marty had been there for her during the weeks she didn't have a job, keeping her properly carbo-fed and offering so much encouragement. She wanted Paul to have that in his life. His parents were wonderful people.

"Listen, can I ask you something?" Nikki asked. "It's...kind of personal."

"Sure. What's, uh, what's on your mind?" Trish's eyes held a bit of worry.

Nikki dropped her gaze to the coffee cup in front of her. "How come I didn't know that Paul was your son?"

Of course Trish loved him. Nikki saw it in the pinch that entered Trish's expression. She glanced away and sighed. "I'm so sorry. I really wanted to tell you; I just couldn't find the right moment." She took a deep breath. "Things have been so strained between Paul and Marty that it's been...well, it's been tough."

"I'd imagine."

"But I knew you'd find out eventually." She brought her smile back and reached for a tray of almond biscotti, offering one to Nikki. "Here."

Awkwardness could always be relieved with sweets. "How can I resist?" Nikki plucked a cookie from the platter.

Trish set the tray down. "Paul actually called last night to say hello."

"He did?"

"Mm-hm. And he had an awful lot of questions about you." She singsonged the last word and leaned closer.

Nikki's heart did a tap dance in her chest. "Really?"

"Oh sure." Trish turned as Marty arrived with a large sheet pan of Italian treats.

"Who we talking about?" he asked.

Nikki said, "Oh, no one," and glanced at Trish, who also said, "No one."

"Mm-hm. Paul. You were talking about Paul."

Nikki couldn't help smiling at the mere mention of his name. "I was just saying how I wasn't even surprised to find out that he was your son."

Marty started stocking the display case with the new pastries. "You weren't surprised?"

Nikki shook her head. "Mm-mm."

"Really. How so?"

Nikki saw her opportunity, and she seized it. "Oh, well, uh, in a lot of ways, I think that he takes after you. You know, he's one of the best chefs in the city, you're the best baker in the city..." She added her most charming smile, hoping Marty would realize that he and Paul had more in common than they thought.

Marty continued working, barely looking at anything but the cannoli. His eyebrows went up. "Glad you think so, but I don't think my son is all that impressed by my baking."

"Wait. Are you kidding? No, he was actually talking about how amazing your almond biscotti are yesterday."

Marty finally paused in his work. "Really?"

"Really." She wanted Marty to know how wonderful Paul was, how delicious his food tasted. "As a cook, he is just so talented." She glanced at Trish, who watched her husband for his reaction.

All he did was lift one eyebrow and slide another cannoli into the case.

Nikki took that as her cue to leave. "Anyway, uh, thanks for this, and I'll see you guys tomorrow." She made eye contact with both Trish and Marty, hoping she hadn't overstepped in her conversation. But she knew what it was like to live far from her family, and Paul and his parents, who both lived right here in Lakeside, should at least try to reconcile. They were more alike than they knew.

She continued to Holly's, already anticipating the dish she was going to make that night after hours. Mashed potato fries, she thought, glad she'd bypassed the heavy carbs this morning so she could indulge that night in buttery mashed potatoes formed into fingerlings and dipped in a batter before hitting the hot oil. After all, Nikki thought, everything was better fried, especially potatoes.

Holly glanced out the window of her kitchen, glad to see the sun peeking through the rainclouds. She looked back at the pan on the stove, in which she'd put peanut butter, root beer, and beef stock. She shook in a few dashes of Worcestershire sauce from the bottle and let the whole thing simmer for a bit, stirring it gently with the wooden spoon, the way she'd seen Nikki do on the surveillance footage.

She lifted the utensil to her lips and blew before taking a taste. All she got was a mouthful of overwhelming peanut flavor. "Ugh. No." She put the pot in the sink and turned on the water to erase the disgusting mixture.

After consulting her notes, she still didn't know what she was doing wrong. Nikki didn't seem to measure anything, and Holly had tried the sauce a half-dozen times without good results. Not even palatable results.

Desperation rose through her throat. Nikki had been cooking every night, and Holly had only mastered one recipe: the ice cream cone chicken. Henry wouldn't wait forever, and she'd need to show him something soon. She wanted to demonstrate the chicken for him and present him with the final, tested recipe of this stew.

She wiped her hand across her forehead. Breathe, she coached herself and went back to her notes. The vegetables, she'd nailed. They waited in a prep bowl. The meat was cut. She just needed to figure out this braising liquid, which was the entire base of the dish.

Holly relaxed as she pressed the garlic this time. She did enjoy cooking, and she thought of her early days in the industry. She had gotten a break from one of the biggest chefs in the business. Memories of Roy Ronaldo's bald head and boisterous laugh filled Holly's mind, and she just let herself cook, not worrying too much about the technicalities of things like tablespoons and dashes.

The sauce bubbled, a nice medium brown color. She braced herself to take another taste. This time, a smile bloomed across her face.

"Yes," she said, spinning to grab the meat from the counter. She placed it in the sauce and put a lid on the pot before returning to her notes.

Ronaldo had taught her to be observant, to take what she could. And Nikki was nobody, not even a trained chef. No one would believe her if she ever found out what Holly had done.

Of course she's going to find out, Holly thought as she turned the page in her notebook. You'll need to find a way to fire her…

The thought sent sadness through her, because Nikki did seem like a nice person. Holly wasn't sure, because she didn't let herself get too close to people, especially not her employees. They needed to see her as the Big Bad Boss and nothing else.

She turned to start a pot of rice, and half an hour later, she served herself the root-beer-braised beef stew—which was every bit as delicious as what Nikki had made.

"A winning recipe," Holly mumbled to herself as she started cleaning up.

Later that night, after she'd put in a full day at the restaurant, Holly took her laptop into her bedroom and got set up. Nikki should be starting her next recipe any moment, as Paul had just flipped off the light and locked up the restaurant.

Sure enough, Nikki entered five minutes later. The woman was like clockwork, bringing in ingredients and prepping the lamb chops with the skill of one trained at the highest culinary institutes.

Holly took notes, surprised by the bar of dark chocolate resting on the board. What was Nikki going to do with that?

She made a parsnip puree and circled it on the

plate. She added drops of the raspberry sauce she'd made, a great pairing for the chops. Those rested in the hot skillet, where Nikki bathed them with herb-infused butter until she deemed them finished.

She placed each lamb chop on top of the puree, creating a beautiful crisscross with the bones. Holly couldn't write fast enough. She leaned forward and took off her glasses, not wanting to miss a single thing.

And then...Nikki reached for that chocolate bar and picked up a carrot peeler. She delicately shaved a few curls of chocolate right onto the hot lamb, where it melted into the meat, creating a type of lamb mole that Holly had never seen.

Would've never thought of.

She laughed and shook her head in disbelief at her incredible luck at finding this assistant, who not only had cleaned up her office and the files, but who had such a talent at thinking outside the box.

Holly wouldn't have time to experiment with the lamb mole, but she reasoned that she didn't need to. Henry would be impressed enough with the ice cream cone chicken—and she was preparing it for him tomorrow at noon.

He'd questioned why he needed to come to her house for the meal, but the lie about not wanting to be in Paul's way in the kitchen had come easily and gone over well.

The following day, she mixed yogurt and honey, crushed cones, and discussed how the sweetness was countered by the tang of the yogurt and the salt she added to the honey. Henry watched, mostly, a surprising action from him. He usually had so much to say, and he spoke so fast.

Holly's heart beat furiously in her chest as she served up the chicken. This was her last chance, and she knew it. Henry knew it. She couldn't even fathom what the newspaper and internet headlines would say if she were forced to close her doors.

She swallowed but beamed at her investor, her confidence in Nikki's recipes still there.

"Well, this is quite a departure from your usual cuisine." He picked up a piece of chicken and took a bite, the crunch from the cones as loud in her kitchen as it had been on the videotape.

He looked at her with surprise and delight. "Oh, wow! Holly, if your new dishes are as good as this one, we don't have anything to worry about." He grinned and went back for another bite.

Relief poured through Holly, and she glanced to the drawer beside the oven where the rest of her notes on Nikki's recipes waited.

Paul spent his days being tormented by Nikki's proximity and doing nothing, saying little, and wondering if she felt different about him since learning his parents were the owners of the bakery.

She'd seemed fond of them and genuinely sorry that Paul didn't get along with his father.

Paul was sorry about it, too, but he didn't know what to do. The idea to create a new dish for Valentine's Day hadn't left him. In fact, it gnawed at him, never leaving, until he finally decided to do something about it.

Last time he'd gone in early to cook, both Holly and Nikki had been there. He didn't want that. He craved the empty kitchen, with nothing between him and his creativity. So he went through his day as normal, listened to Jerrod's whispers about asking Angela out, and went home to his sterile apartment at night.

But he didn't head to bed like normal. Oh, no. Tonight, he was returning to the kitchen, an idea percolating about pork and blueberries.

When he arrived back at the restaurant, he noticed the light in the kitchen was still on. Just a splash of it fell around the corner and into the dining room, but it was enough to put Paul on alert.

He knew he'd turned out that light, and it was too early for the cleaning crew to be here. Had Holly come back?

He slowed, not wanting to run into her. He didn't have the mental fortitude to argue this late at night— or early in the morning, depending on how he looked at it.

The scent of butter and sugar met his nose. Someone was in the kitchen cooking. *His* kitchen.

He moved forward with more speed now, not bothering to be quiet. A few steps from the corner, the light went out, causing his heart to skip several beats. Did they really think they could hide from him?

His next thought was about the many and varied tools in the kitchen the other person had at their disposal. Pans, sheet trays, knives...

He rounded the corner and flipped on the light anyway. No one jumped out at him, but someone had been here because the stove was still on, a pot still boiling on the burner. "Hello?" he called.

Nikki half-stood from behind the end of the counter, a huge cast-iron skillet in her hand.

Paul's heartbeat went nuts now, and only a little bit because of the way she wielded the skillet like a baseball bat.

She wore that beautiful red shirt, as if she hadn't gone home yet, and she seemed as perky and lively as she had twelve hours ago. He liked seeing her—but what was she doing here? Now?

He swept his eyes along the counter covered with ingredients, the stove with the bubbling pots. When he looked back at her, she was still only slightly raised from behind the counter.

"Hi! Paul!" Nikki straightened and came out from her hiding place.

He frowned at the same time he smiled, unsure of how to greet her.

She edged around the counter, that cast-iron skillet still clenched firmly in her hand. "Hi, uh, you scared me half to death." She approached but didn't put the pan down.

He lifted his hand in surrender. "Believe me, it wasn't intentional."

She shook the pan at him, that playful smile that he loved on her face. "You know, I almost flattened your head with a skillet."

"Well, maybe next time, go for the rolling pin." He grinned at her, his confusion over her presence still igniting his bloodstream.

She chortled and set the skillet on the flattop, which didn't appear to be lit. "What are you doing sneaking around anyway?"

"I wouldn't call coming into my place of employment sneaking around."

"Point taken." She leaned her hip into the counter, and Paul realized he had his two favorite things standing right in front of him—his kitchen and Nikki.

He pulled his keys out of his coat pocket. "Also, I have a key."

"So do I." She said it like it was no big deal, like every member of Holly's staff had a key.

But Paul knew they didn't. He leaned one hand onto the counter and put the other on his waist. "You have a key? Why would Holly give you a key?"

Something was going on here. Something fishy—and not the good kind of fish like salmon or grouper. His anxiety lifted one rung as Nikki's silence went on and on.

"Because she likes me. A lot." Nikki wasn't a very good liar.

Paul circled her, checking out what she had simmering on the stove—definitely the butter and sugar he'd smelled out in the dining room. "It took her two years to give me one." He turned back to Nikki, his impatience growing. "What is going on here?"

She faced him, her expression earnest. She gave a sigh that broadcasted that she'd been caught and she knew it, was frustrated about it. Her wide, eager eyes now raced with a trace of panic.

"I gave my word I wouldn't say anything," she said.

This wasn't happening. He liked this woman and she was keeping secrets from him? Right here in his own kitchen!

"You gave your word you wouldn't say anything? Come on, what's going on?"

"I—" She looked away, evading his even gaze, and sighed. At least he'd been right about her not saying something about Jerrod and Angela.

"Holly just lets me cook after hours," she finally said in a rush of words.

His muscles seized. Was Holly going to replace him with Nikki? "Why?" He smiled and laughed, his nerves getting the best of him.

"Because she found out that I'm a cook, and well, for whatever reason, she told me to have fun and do my thing."

Paul knew there was a reason, and Nikki didn't seem too concerned about what it was. But Paul was. When it came to Holly, she didn't do anything without a good reason. Heck, a great reason.

And there was absolutely *no* reason for her to let Nikki cook in her kitchen using not-free ingredients. Holly's heart didn't beat like that.

"Well, it looks like your 'thing' is about to boil over." He waved to the pot behind him, which he could hear starting to sizzle hot liquid on an even hotter metal burner.

Nikki glanced over, her face flashing with disbelief. She rushed past him, almost pushing right into him. "Oh, sorry. Sorry."

He couldn't help the wide smile that came across his face. He liked teasing Nikki, loved her emphatic reactions, and enjoyed spending time with her.

At the same time, he'd come here to cook, and now he'd have to clean up before he could even start. Maybe she'd cook beside him. That thought appealed to him greatly.

He turned to find her stirring furiously as if she could salvage the mess. "It looks interesting."

"It looks awful! Awful is the word that you are looking for to describe that." She left the wooden spoon in the gooey mess and approached him, half-laughing along with her words.

He chuckled as she pointed at him. "Okay, listen, don't judge me. I was just, you know, experimenting with savory and sweet, so I threw in a cup of kettle corn, and well, as you can see, the sugar caramelized and burnt." At least she could admit she wasn't perfect. She clapped and beamed at him, causing Paul's heart to twist dangerously. If he wasn't careful, he'd find himself in the same situation as Jerrod.

His mind spun, and he really wanted to know if she had a boyfriend. That would change a lot of things, but he couldn't just blurt out that question. It would give away too much, too soon.

"You gonna go for round two?" He really hoped she'd stay.

"No, no. I've had enough upsets for one night. So the kitchen's all yours. I'm assuming that's why you snuck in?" She edged closer to him, her chest nearly pressing into his.

Paul breathed in the scent of her skin—powdery and soft—and also got a noseful of the burnt sugar. "I came in to try out something new of my own for Valentine's Day. Thought this one might meet Holly's approval."

"Oh, well, mind if I stick around?" She seemed eager to stay, and he hoped it wasn't so she could critique his cooking technique, but because she liked him as much as he liked her.

"I'd like that." He grinned, and she returned it. He traded his coat for an apron and went into the walk-in to get a package of pork chops and one of blueberries he'd hidden there just before dinner service. He'd use Holly's kitchen and her spices, but he didn't want to jeopardize his career by assuming he could use anything he wanted from the fridge.

He knew better than that. Though, as he caught Nikki watching him, he wondered why she'd been able to use whatever she wanted from Holly's supply. Yes, Holly was definitely up to something, and someone as kind as Nikki didn't even question what.

She'd probably let someone use her ingredients and kitchen, no questions asked.

But Paul knew Holly better than that, and there was something going on after hours in this kitchen that didn't add up.

Chapter thirteen

Holly was late getting to the computer that night. Didn't matter. She could go back and watch the videos whenever she wanted. She found she liked to watch Nikki in real time, only because it was invigorating to witness the woman cook live.

But tonight, she'd stopped by the bookstore, just to see if they still had her latest cookbook in stock. They did, but only one copy, and it was shoved between two of some other celebrity chef's books.

So she'd inconspicuously taken it out and placed it cover-out on top of their endcap display.

She opened the laptop and went to change into her pajamas while it connected to the internet. When she returned, there was more than one voice on the screen. She picked up her notebook and advanced toward the laptop, shock traveling through her at what she saw.

Paul.

Paul was in the kitchen with Nikki, and they were

talking about pork chops, blueberries, and balsamic glazes.

Holly stared, not wanting to believe what she was seeing. She'd always known she'd have to fire Nikki in order to use the recipes. But Paul?

He'd been with her since the restaurant had opened five years ago. Her heart twisted in her chest. She'd never seen Paul on any of the other videos, but there he was, live and in color.

She peered closer, because it looked like what he was doing was pretty interesting.

Stop it, she told herself. She had the new recipes she needed, and she also needed Paul to execute them. Maybe she could still salvage this and keep him.

Nikki had always enjoyed her time in the kitchen with other cooks. Of course, she'd always been the head cook, able to direct others as she put up chili, sandwiches, and pancakes.

But being in the kitchen with Paul brought a whole new charge to cooking. Or maybe that was just the spark between them. No matter what, she enjoyed talking to him about food, watching him cook—the man had serious skills with proteins, vegetables, fruits, and sauces—and simply being in the same space as him.

"So should we try it?" He glanced at her after making his plates immaculate.

"Of course." She followed him around the corner and into the dining room. He grinned at her as he sat beside her. He waited until she took the first bite. The tanginess from the fruit combined so well with the sour balsamic and the tender pork.

"Holly would be crazy not to like this. It's perfect for Valentine's Day." The sauce had a deep purple hue, which screamed romance to Nikki way more than any of that gaudy pink stuff she'd seen around town.

"I was thinking maybe to do it as a pork loin instead of a pork chop so it could be shared. You know, a lot of couples like to come in for a romantic meal and order for two."

Nikki grinned even though her chest tightened. She leaned back in her chair and took a sip of wine. "Yeah, I understand the concept. I just don't practice it much."

"What, ordering for two?"

"No, the romantic-meal part."

"Yeah, I hear you. Being in the restaurant business doesn't leave you much time for a personal life." He lifted his powerful shoulders in a shrug.

Nikki had never minded her single status when she worked as a cook, but she agreed with a casual giggle. "Not to mention the fact that manning a grill all day makes a chef smell like grease." She personally liked the scent of a man after he'd been working in the kitchen, and the flirtatious look she gave Paul probably said so.

"So, no boyfriend?"

Why he'd gone straight to that, she wasn't sure. But she said, "No, no boyfriend." She hoped maybe he was looking to take the job, but he didn't inch toward her and had never once tried to hold her hand as they'd walked through the park last weekend. Nothing but that intense interest in his eyes. The physical barrier between them hadn't been broken yet, and everything strained in Nikki to touch him. Crack that ice.

"I had a serious relationship two years ago," she said to further explain, to keep talking, prolonging the moment. "But we worked together, and it just got too messy."

"I can totally relate. I once dated a fellow chef, and after a disagreement, she sabotaged my Bolognese with an entire jar of cayenne pepper."

Nikki laughed and glanced away, wondering what she was doing. Was she saying she didn't want to date him because they worked together? Pushing him away because of Holly's rules? Or testing him to see if he wanted to forget about the rules and ask her out?

"That experience definitely taught me never to date someone that I work with," he said, and Nikki's hopes crashed to the floor. He didn't even smile when he said it.

She finished running her hand through her hair— her standard flirtation gesture—and said, "Yeah, better not to complicate work and personal life."

But the way he looked at her said otherwise, and she couldn't help feeling another moment between them. A powerful moment, where they both existed at the same time and somehow, understood each other perfectly.

And she knew. He liked her just as much as she liked him, no matter what he said about not dating someone he worked with. Besides, it wasn't like they were both chefs in the same kitchen or anything.

He broke the moment first and looked away. "So." He gave a small chuckle, and he really did have a killer smile. "What happened with you and your ex-boyfriend?"

"Well," she said, hoping she wouldn't break into babbling. *Just a few sentences.*

"For starters, we just weren't really a good fit. But mostly, he just didn't support my dreams. And it hurt." It still did, though she didn't know why. She hadn't thought about Ryan in a long time, and she wasn't interested in getting back together with him.

"So what are your dreams?"

"To open up a place like this one day." She glanced around Holly Hanson's like it was Disneyland, her face brightening. But even as she drank in the beautiful furniture and the high-end carpets, she knew she didn't want a restaurant like Holly's. It was too fancy. She'd loved working at Gus's, but she didn't want a diner, either. There had to be something in the middle where the two met—that was what Nikki wanted.

She'd tried explaining that to Ryan, but he'd been

disinterested from the start. She should've been able to recognize those red flags, but she'd ignored them.

"You know," she said, not really sure why she needed to vocalize any more. After all, her "few sentences" had already been said. "Looking back, I guess deep down, I always knew we weren't a match. I just wasn't really honest with myself. Anyhow, weeks turned into months, months turned into a year, Valentine's Day rolled around, and he took me out to dinner."

She wasn't sure why she was telling him all this. Maybe it was her mouth turning to babble mode again. Or maybe because he seemed genuinely interested in knowing, that he really seemed to care about her.

"I was certain he was going to propose," she said. "But...he broke up with me." The pain gushing through her was as real now as it had been two years ago. This was why she'd rather skip the whole month of February.

"On Valentine's Day?"

"Yeah. So it's safe to say I'm not really a Valentine's Day person." She tried to chuckle but it didn't come off right.

He picked up his wine glass. "Well, here's to us single chefs around the world. May we find companionship in the food that we prepare."

She lifted her glass also. "To the food that we prepare." They clinked glasses, and Nikki thought things couldn't get any more perfect. Sure, maybe she would've liked this meal to end in an invitation to another one—on Valentine's Day—but she'd take a couple of hours with Paul in the dead of night any day of the week.

She sipped her wine and had barely swallowed when Holly said, "What a beautiful meal you're sharing."

Nikki hastily set down her glass, panic spiking through her. "Oh, did the alarm go off?" There were plenty sounding inside her. From the dark look on Holly's face, this wasn't going to end well.

"We were just cooking—" Paul tried.

Holly came out of the darkness and into the light. "You just decided to make yourself a nice romantic dinner for two." She scanned the remains of the food in front of them.

"Romantic? No, not at all." Nikki didn't know how to say this in front of Paul without hurting his feelings.

"Nikki, I was very clear about the terms of our agreement. I trusted you, and you betrayed my trust." She punctuated certain words with her hands, making Nikki feel about two inches tall. Was it her fault Paul had come in after hours?

What would Holly have told him if she'd been here and Paul had walked in?

A lie, Nikki thought, the first crack in her absolute allegiance to Holly seeping through her subconscious. She shook her head. No. Holly was a reasonable person, not a diva.

"And Paul," Holly continued. "How in the world

is it possible that you think it's appropriate to have a date on my dime, after hours, in my restaurant?"

Paul shook his head in disbelief and rose to his feet, clearly angry. "Holly, there's nothing inappropriate going on here."

Nikki stood, too, taking her cues from Paul. "Holly, if you'd just let me explain—" She glanced at him, but he glared at Holly without flinching.

"I'm gonna make this easy on all of us." She put her hands on her hips. "You're both fired."

The air left Nikki's lungs, and she couldn't say anything.

"Are you serious?" Paul sounded beyond shocked.

"Very." Holly didn't even look upset. Worried. Scared. Nothing.

No one moved, and Nikki wasn't sure she even could. Her brain was screaming at her about her bag in the back, the mess they'd left in the kitchen, and the key to the restaurant she used every night to let herself out after she finished cooking.

What was she to do about all of that?

But Holly wasn't moving, and she certainly hadn't been kidding. Nikki stared at her, sure she wasn't as bad as Angela had made her sound, sure her previous three assistants had just been unfit for the job. But now...now she wasn't so sure.

Paul exhaled and reached for his coat. "C'mon, Nikki. We've just been liberated." He stepped past her, and Nikki stared at Holly in disbelief. Still, no words came, and that was saying something.

She followed Paul because she had no other choice. Her mind felt numb; her feet moved without direction from her brain.

The door nearly slammed closed behind her, a very final punctuation mark to her firing. After she'd joined Paul on the sidewalk, she asked, "Can you figure out what just happened in there?"

"Other than the fact we were both just fired?" He waved at the closed door in frustration. He looked up the street and then down. "No. Here. Come on." He draped his coat around her shoulders as their breath steamed in the air in front of them.

She'd left her coat behind, and she really loved that jacket. Apprehension pulled through her at having to go back and retrieve her things. Holly wouldn't throw them away, would she?

Previously, Nikki couldn't imagine her doing that. But everything seemed to be up in the air at the moment.

"Thanks." She held on to the collar of the coat to keep it from slipping from her shoulders as they walked. "I can't help but feel this whole thing is all my fault. I'm so sorry, Paul."

"You shouldn't be. I'm the one who has history with Holly. I'm sure that her anger was just directed at me. You were just in the wrong place at the wrong time." He seemed flustered, barely able to put his thoughts together. She'd never realized he spoke so much with his hands, but now he gestured with almost every word.

He scoffed and turned back toward the restaurant. "What was she doing in the restaurant tonight? She never comes in after hours." He looked so broken, so lost.

Nikki paused on the sidewalk in front of him. "It's not like we can go back in there and ask her."

"I guess it doesn't matter. My head is spinning." He touched his forehead, turned, and walked away, his obvious distress filling Nikki with remorse.

She felt the same way he did. She'd just gotten this job and had barely collected her first paycheck. "Yeah. Mine, too."

Chapter Fourteen

Nikki slept poorly. It was late by the time she got home anyway, and all she could see was Paul's tortured face as he'd walked away from the restaurant where he'd been employed for the past five years.

In the morning, Angela met her in the kitchen, thankfully, with a pot of hot coffee. "What's wrong with you?" Of course Ang would know just by looking. Nikki had purposefully avoided the mirror so she wouldn't have to see herself so disheveled.

"Holly fired us."

"Us?"

"Me and Paul." Nikki collapsed at the bar while Angela poured her a cup of coffee. With her favorite stoneware and enough sugar, maybe Nikki could make it through today. The story of what had happened the previous night slipped out word by miserable word. Nikki had hoped she'd feel better after telling the tale, but she didn't.

Paul had worked there for five years. *Five years.* And she'd caused him to lose his job in a single night. She thought firing him because she'd told Paul about the late-night sessions in the kitchen was extreme. No way he should've lost his job over it. He probably went in all the time and tried out new recipes. Holly hadn't fired him over the heart-shaped ravioli.

None of it made sense, and Nikki laid her head in her hands as Angela patted her shoulder. "I told you she was a diva. I mean, who acts like that after she gave you permission to use the kitchen?"

Nikki couldn't answer, and she hated the idea that Holly wasn't the nice, kind, well-meaning boss who wanted to give Nikki her big break.

Ang went to get ready for work, leaving Nikki alone in the silent apartment. She felt far from herself, and she didn't like it. She wanted to cook, and even being Holly Hanson's assistant hadn't quenched that thirst.

Cooking in that professional kitchen with expensive equipment and top-quality ingredients had. But she didn't have the money to buy her own place or attend culinary school.

So go do what you can do, she told herself, hoping she could pick herself up from this disaster and move on.

Nikki shook her head as she brushed her teeth, creating a weird back and forth sensation in her head. Ang texted that Holly hadn't come in yet, so Nikki should hurry over and slip into the restaurant to retrieve her belongings. Her pulse beat double time at the prospect of seeing Holly. And it wasn't the good kind of pounding in excitement, the way it had been when she'd wanted to meet her idol, but a dread-filled kind that made her sad as well as anxious.

The loss of Holly as her mentor—even if she'd never actually taught her anything—cut Nikki to the core. She'd placed Holly on such a high pedestal. She fingered the key to the restaurant in her pocket and left the apartment. She even bypassed Delucci's, not wanting to face Trish and Marty. She didn't trust herself and her loose tongue to keep the news of Paul's lost job a secret. He should get to tell them, and Nikki didn't like being the bearer of bad news.

Hurry. Angela's text came when Nikki was only a block from the restaurant, and she increased her pace so she wouldn't miss her opportunity to get in and out without seeing Holly.

She made it to the restaurant, which was still closed, and therefore, locked. She didn't dare use her key in case Holly had some sort of electronic tracker on it, so she peered in the window for Angela and didn't see her. "Come on."

Angela came rushing out from the back and waved for her to come in. She opened the door and Nikki slipped into the restaurant.

"The coast is clear. Holly's gone."

"I'm just gonna grab my bag, and then I'll be out." She gave Angela a grateful smile. "Okay. I'll be quick."

They hurried through the dining room to the office in the back. Nikki's heart sprinted through her chest, sure Holly would arrive at any moment and verbally berate her again.

Angela stood watch at the door, keeping it partially open. "Go, go, go, go. Quick, quick."

Nikki started out toward the hooks where she'd hung her things, stepping over to the desk to set the key there. She was just going to turn back, then grab her bag. But something on Holly's desk snagged her attention.

A huge folder with the words NEW MENU across the front of it.

She paused. "New menu?" She opened the folder and saw a beautiful, professionally designed menu on one side and a recipe clipped on the other. "What?"

Her recipe.

Her recipe for peanut butter root beer Bourguignon.

"No." Her head started shaking. "No way."

"What?" Angela turned from her post at the door, but Nikki couldn't see farther than the words on the menu.

She read down the list, her voice getting angrier and angrier with every word she saw. "Peanut butter root beer Bourguignon, waffle fried chicken, lamb mole! Sound familiar?" She whipped her attention to Angela.

"Yeah, those sound like your recipes."

"They are my recipes." She'd never felt so…upset. Unsettled. Angry. No, furious. Tears pricked her eyes, and she blinked them back, trying to find something to focus on.

Her gaze landed on Holly's computer, which had a stilled image on it—of her.

She leaned forward. "I can't believe this!" She hit play and saw herself plating the lamb mole from several nights ago.

"Surveillance footage?" Angela joined her at the desk, completely abandoning her post. "Why would she record you?"

"Because she's stealing my recipes." Nikki thought she was going to throw up. Right now. And then Holly would know she'd been there. Unable to see straight, she grabbed her bag from the hook and slammed the blue folder containing her recipes and the new menu closed.

"I have to go." She saw Angela's tortured expression as she brushed past her. "See you at home."

Nikki strode down the street, bypassing the vibrant downtown area in favor of the quieter park where she and Paul had walked.

Paul.

Holly had fired him because he was in the wrong place at the wrong time. She knew now that Holly would've gotten rid of her sooner or later. After all, she couldn't start serving Nikki's recipes while she was still an employee.

Bitterness coated her throat, and she couldn't swallow it away no matter how hard she tried.

Her phone chimed, and she checked it. Paul. *What are you doing today?*

She didn't want to tell him she was on the verge of tears. Didn't want him to know about the stolen recipes—then he'd blame her for the loss of his executive chef job. And she simply couldn't bear to lose him, too.

So she pocketed her phone and stared past the playground where moms sat on benches while their kids slid down slides and swung back and forth on swings. She thought of her own mother and what she might say if Nikki called with this bad news.

Oh, I'm so sorry, honey. What are you going to do now?

"I don't know, Mom," Nikki whispered to herself. And she was tired of not knowing. Tired of not being able to do what she loved and was really good at. Tired of keeping all the negative things to herself instead of letting her parents help her.

So she did something she'd never done before. She pulled out her phone and dialed her mom, intending to tell her something that was less than great.

"Mom," she said when her mother answered. Nikki's emotion swam so close to the surface she couldn't keep it out of her voice.

"Nik, what's going on?" Just the sound of her mom's voice soothed her.

Nikki sighed, turning away from the joviality on the playground in favor of the open grass, which was mostly empty. "I lost my job, and I need a new one."

"Lost your job? Oh, honey, I'm so sorry."

Nikki couldn't help the smile that curved her mouth. What she'd imagined her mom saying and what she'd said were almost identical.

"It's really unfair, actually," Nikki said, a sense of indignation overcoming her. She spilled the whole story to her mom, and that relief she'd hoped would come as she talked to Angela finally arrived.

She heaved a deep breath in and then out. "So." That was all she could say, because "so" about summed up where she was.

"You'll find something," her mom said. "Just like you always have."

Nikki felt tired from head to toe. She didn't want to just find something. She wanted her own restaurant. But with her mother's tips and her father's middle-class income, they weren't in a position to help her. And the way she couldn't keep a job meant she could barely support herself.

"Thanks, Mom," Nikki said. "I'll keep you updated." She ended the call because she didn't want to drag out the drama. She'd told her mom about Gus's Kitchen closing, but not until she'd secured the job at

Holly Hanson's. So her mom didn't know Nikki had seriously considered becoming a dog walker.

Another text came in, this time from Angela. *You okay? I'm worried about you.*

Was Nikki okay? She wasn't entirely sure, but she texted, *Yeah, I'm okay.*

Paul says he can't get ahold of you.

Nikki glanced away from her phone. She should call Paul. She just wanted a little more time before she told him the real reason why Holly had let her use the kitchen after hours.

Is he at the restaurant?

No, Jerrod is getting messages from him. Holly is unpleasant today, but we're managing to grab a few seconds to talk.

Of course Paul wouldn't be at the restaurant, though he had a key, too. But it wouldn't be unreasonable for him to go back there and tie off the loose ends.

I'm okay, she sent again, wandering across the lawn and finding a bench by the skeleton of a tree. She sat, taking the time to just enjoy a few minutes outside, breathe in the fresh air, and wonder where her next opportunity would come from.

When Nikki made it back to her apartment, darkness had already fallen. She went up the stairs into the kitchen and hung up her coat. Her eyes drifted to the menus on the wall.

She deserved another one. A great big, giant-sized

poster of Holly Hanson's with her recipes, her food, on the menu.

The injustice of it all engulfed her, and Nikki turned to the only thing she could control at the moment.

Angela returned just after eleven, her footsteps coming up to the kitchen where Nikki was still awake.

"Oh. Should've known you'd be cleaning." Angela sounded sorry and upbeat at the same time, her usual demeanor. "You're always cleaning when you're upset."

Nikki scrubbed the saltshaker with the toothbrush a little harder. Back and forth. Back and forth. Every surface could be cleaner. It really could, and Nikki could control it.

"I've cleaned all of these twice already." She glanced down the row of vintage kitchen equipment she'd already scrubbed. She gave Angela a sideways look. "You're home early." She froze and turned to her friend. "Wait, did Holly fire you, too?"

"No, no. She did give the staff the week off, though." She looked uncomfortable, and Nikki went back to her cleaning. She was trying not to care what was happening at Holly Hanson's.

"They're doing renovations at the restaurant," Angela continued. "She's going to re-open with the new menu...right after Valentine's Day."

Nikki swung her attention toward Angela, who looked pained, aghast. She made a face. "Actually... your menu."

Nikki inhaled deliberately, trying to figure out how to keep her emotions inside. She didn't understand why Holly had taken advantage of her. Not only was Holly a thief, but she was also a liar. She'd loved Nikki's beef stew, but with a restaurant as upscale as hers, she'd renamed it.

Bourguignon.

As if.

That was carrots, onions, celery, and beef in a savory-sweet broth. It was a stew—classic diner food. Maybe a bit more upscale than diner food, but certainly not a Bourguignon.

Stupid, fancy trained chefs, she thought. They were always trying to make things sound better than they actually were. Then Holly could charge twenty-nine dollars for the meal instead of fifteen.

As if an azure crayon was somehow better at making art than a blue one. That "Bourguignon" didn't taste any better than her "beef stew."

Nikki glanced to the tower of cookbooks sitting on the ottoman a few feet away. She'd loved her cookbooks for years, creating from them and enjoying the fancy names of the foods inside.

Now they all seemed ridiculous, especially Holly's cookbooks, which sat in a stack because Nikki had been looking at them earlier this week.

How many of those recipes were actually Holly's? After all, if she was willing to put stolen recipes on her restaurant's menu and expect to get away with it, Nikki couldn't believe any of the recipes in the book could really be hers.

She didn't want them even if they were authentic. Time to clean this place up. She marched past Angela, her footsteps ringing in the apartment as she picked up the cookbooks and ceremoniously dumped them in the trash can.

When Nikki texted Paul and asked if he wanted to meet at the farmers' market and then help at the community center luncheon, he said yes. And not only because he didn't have anything to do that day.

He'd texted her several times the previous day, and she hadn't answered. He'd worried that she blamed him for the loss of her job, but no matter how he spun the situation, he wasn't sure it was his fault.

He didn't blame her either—she wasn't at fault for cooking when Holly had given her permission to do so.

No, this firing was just classic Holly Hanson. Unpredictable. Unstable. Unrealistic.

After all, did she really think someone could just step into his shoes? He'd run her kitchen since the day the restaurant had opened, and there wasn't a chef on her staff right now that could do half of what he did.

Part of him wanted to find a big hat, sneak into the restaurant that night, and see what came out of the kitchen when he wasn't there.

He was tired of thinking about those few moments before Holly had said, "You're fired," but he was relieved Nikki was talking to him again. He wasn't sure why she hadn't yesterday, but he intended to find out when he saw her at the farmers' market.

She wasn't wearing her pink coat today, but a black wool one that made her hair look like a shiny penny. Paul fought the urge to touch it and instead stuffed his gloved hands into his pockets though the weather was starting to thaw.

"Hey," he said, sidling up to her at the citrus stand, where she held three limes in her hand.

"Hey, yourself." She gave him her trademark smile, and he relaxed further.

"What's on the menu today?"

"Corn and clam chowder," Nikki said. "I made it one night at Holly's, and I didn't see it on the menu. Maybe she couldn't recreate it." She shrugged and moved down to start picking out ears of fresh corn. "But the people at the community center are going to get a taste of it first. I can tell you that."

Paul didn't know what to say to soothe Nikki. When she'd called as soon as he'd confirmed their meeting to tell him Holly had stolen her recipes and would be re-launching the restaurant just after Valentine's Day, he hadn't known what to tell her. He still didn't.

But Nikki had plenty, and he just let her talk, knowing that she released her steam through her mouth while he bottled things up and then avoided the situation for years. He honestly wasn't sure which method was better. Neither of them seemed to be achieving what they needed to.

Nikki paid for the produce and they left the farmers' market. "I just don't understand how she can have the entire world in her hands and then rip off someone who's struggling." Nikki carried a distasteful look on her face. "It's not right. I mean, it isn't fair." She gestured with her hand as if the man passing by was at fault.

"I always knew Holly could go low," Paul said. "But I never thought she'd go that low." He hated that he hadn't had time to figure out what Holly had been up to.

"Hey, listen." She turned back to him, most of her negativity gone. "Um, I have to head to your parents' bakery to pick up some dinner rolls. You want to come with me?" She paused and brushed her hair over her shoulder.

Paul wanted to go with her. Almost anywhere with her. He glanced up and down the street, searching for an excuse and not finding one. "Uh...I think I'll pass."

She looked disappointed, and he hated doing that to her.

"Listen, Paul, um, I've been thinking about your relationship with your dad."

He sighed and looked away. He didn't need her to analyze him, offer solutions, or even spend any time thinking about the tattered relationship. He watched a couple walk by as she continued.

"And it seems like maybe you two just need to talk it out. Seems like you both feel misunderstood."

"Misunderstood." He nodded like he couldn't believe anyone would really think that. He finally looked at her again. "Do you know he has never even tried anything I've made?"

Nikki wore a sorrowful expression, but Paul didn't need that, either. She probably cooked for her parents every Thanksgiving and Christmas, and they were probably like everyone else in this town—complimenting her for how great her food tasted.

Paul didn't begrudge her that, but he simply didn't enjoy the same luxury. "It's probably for the best. He can be really judgmental."

"No, you're an amazing chef. I'm sure he'd love anything that you cooked." Her positivity usually lifted his spirits. Today, though, it didn't have its usual oomph.

"Look, Nikki, the relationship between me and my father, it's—it's complicated. I know you're just trying to help, but I'd rather you not get involved. Okay?"

She ducked her head, said, "Sure," and they continued toward the community center. He mused silently on the conversation, hoping he hadn't been too rude to her. But he always found it better to be forthcoming about things, and he really didn't want her getting in the middle of his family's business.

He knew his mom had suffered by being stuck between him and his father, and he didn't want to do that to Nikki.

So he stayed at the center while she went to the bakery without him. She returned in good spirits, and he wondered what his parents had said to her. She didn't say anything, didn't pester him about going with her or say that they'd missed him.

He worked on a garlic cheese biscuit to go with the soup, and Beth, the center's director, made three salad dressings to put on the bar Nikki had put together with the produce from the farmers' market.

He liked working in this low-pressure venue, liked helping people who came through to get fed, liked feeling that what he was doing actually mattered.

Lunch ended, and he started to help clean up by going out among the tables and picking up the trash. He cleared one table and moved to another as someone said something. He wasn't looking when he reached for the plate, and his hand touched Nikki's.

A flame shot up his arm, and she pulled her fingers away with a shy smile he returned. They took their dishes to the bin where Beth stood, a wide grin on her face for the people she helped.

When she noticed Paul and Nikki, she said, "Paul, we can't thank you enough for helping out today."

He put his dishes in the bin. "Happy to do it again.

My schedule is suddenly wide open." He smiled, but there was no joy behind it. He didn't think he'd have any problem finding another job. Problem was, he wasn't sure he wanted to go cook for someone else. He was a chef, and he wanted to be more of the creative force for the food at a restaurant. And in order to do that, he needed to be the chef-owner.

Beth beamed at him and then turned her attention to Nikki, who seemed a bit subdued. She wasn't worried about him, was she? Maybe she felt guilty over him getting fired, but he'd assured her several times that it wasn't her fault.

"Nikki, a really great meal again. Everyone loved it."

"Thanks, Beth. Well, Paul was a huge help, too." She met his eye, and he couldn't resist smiling at her. He wanted her to be happy, but he didn't know how to help her beyond spending their day "off" together so she wouldn't feel alone.

"You know, you really need to get your own restaurant," Beth said. "It would be a big hit, I'm telling you." She lifted the bin of dishes and left Nikki alone with Paul.

"She is right, you know."

She'd wanted her own place for a long time, while the idea was still in its infancy inside Paul's mind.

Nikki nodded, indicating she'd heard him, but her gaze wandered across the few people who still lingered at the tables. A group of them drank from to-go cups, probably hot chocolate.

Paul searched for some reason he needed to stay with her. Maybe they could go to dinner together. They weren't co-workers with strange rules about who they could date anymore. He was just about to ask her to dinner when Nikki blurted, "A pop-up. Hot chocolate."

He frowned, and she hurried around the table and stared at the still-sipping people. "Hey, you remember that place that we got the hot chocolate from? The pop-up?"

"Yeah." He wasn't quite following her train of thought, and he hoped she'd slow down and let him on.

She looked up at him, a sense of wonder lighting her eyes. "What if, we opened up…"

Paul suddenly got it. "A pop-up," he said with her.

"Right?" She looked at him, clearly waiting for him to validate her. His mind spun, rotating around what it would take to find the space, get the deposit, the décor, the menu…

He blinked and lifted his mouth into half a smile. "I think you're onto something here, Nik." The nickname flowed easily from his mouth, and she didn't seem to mind at all.

"I mean, all we have to do is find a space."

"That's closed down or vacant. Has a really good kitchen."

"I know just the spot." Of course she did. When Nikki had ideas, they usually already had some legs. Paul liked that about her, and when she hastened to untie her apron, he did the same, anxious to know where this perfect spot was.

Chapter Fifteen

Nikki's excitement grew with every step she took. She babbled to Paul, who simply let her talk about the pop-up shop she wanted to do, the menu, the décor, all of it. None of it made sense, because she really had no idea how to do this. She didn't know where to order food, supplies, or any of it.

But she knew where the pop-up could be located.

She rounded the corner and the huge red sign that read GUS'S KITCHEN came into view. She stalled, her breath coming in bursts from the quick march over here from the community center.

"Gus's," she said, turning to Paul to see if he agreed.

"Gus's." He nodded, his eyes shining like they were made of glass.

They continued toward the space, and Nikki knew this was going to work out. She'd called Gus and asked him to meet her down at the Kitchen before leaving the center, and sure enough, he greeted them at the door.

"Okay, so we have an idea." She exchanged a glance with Paul, who gestured for her to explain it. So Nikki did.

"Pop-up what?" Gus asked.

"Just think of it as a rental," Nikki said. "We'll lease the space for three days, and then we'll return it just as we found it." Her nerves were getting the better of her, because the urge to ramble was strong. She pushed it back, swallowed, and waited for Gus's verdict.

"Well, you don't hear anyone banging on the door, wanting to take it over."

"So, that's a yes?"

"Yes, indeed."

Paul chuckled, and Nikki flew into Gus's arms. "Thank you, Gus!"

"We'll go to the bank and get your deposit right away," Paul said, relief evident in his expression.

"Oh, there's no rush. This all sounds very exciting, you two." Gus walked away, and Nikki surveyed the space, her excitement up near the clouds now.

"This is fantastic," she said, her heart near exploding. "It's the perfect way for me to try my own thing but start small." She sobered the teensiest bit. "We just have to open before Holly Hanson's re-opening, so everyone knows those recipes are mine and not hers."

Which meant they had about a week to get this place up and running. Her excitement plummeted as she realized how much work she had ahead of her—of them—if they were going to pull this off.

"Maybe we could invite some food critics," Paul said, a charming smile on his face.

"Food critics?" Nikki flirted right on back. "But you hate food critics."

He shrugged and exhaled, never taking his eyes from her. She wasn't sure what he meant by that, but she just said, "Okay, great. It's perfect."

The first thing she needed to do was get some extra hands on deck. And she knew just who to call.

Jerrod and Angela, who both had the week off because of Holly Hanson's remodel.

"What days were you thinking?" Paul asked as they walked to the bank to get the deposit for Gus.

"Let's do Valentine's Day." Nikki walked with a definite bounce in her step, and they stopped by a party supply store to get some red, pink, and white paper for the décor. She made sure to put in some purple, too—the understated Valentine's Day color.

By the time they returned to Gus's Kitchen, Jerrod and Angela stood on the sidewalk out front, and Nikki swore she saw them holding hands before they stepped apart and greeted her and Paul.

They went inside and got to work transforming the paper and ribbon into hearts fit for a Valentine's Day pop-up restaurant. Paul opened the red paper lanterns, and Angela and Jerrod quibbled over where the beads should go.

Nikki reveled in the charged atmosphere, and she left them to the decorations while she started sketching out the menu. After a few minutes, Paul wandered over to join her, and she basked in the heat from his body, the masculine scent of his cologne.

Her day ended so much differently than it had begun that Nikki felt like each half had existed in two separate universes. She and Paul agreed to meet the next morning to finalize the menu, and Angela promised she'd work on the social media aspect of the pop-up shop so they could get the news out about it.

Nikki fell into bed for the second night in a row, but tonight, her exhaustion was born from an emotional high instead of the lowest moment of her life.

The following day, Paul mentally coached himself all the way to Nikki's. First, the fact that he was going to her home to finalize the menu had his insides all knotted up. They weren't dating, but the shy touches, the quick smiles, and the flirting had certainly increased every time they were together.

Without Holly's insane no-dating-each-other policy, Paul was free to ask Nikki to dinner. He wasn't going to, though, because neither of them would have time as they prepared to open their Valentine's Day-themed pop-up restaurant in only four days.

And then there was all that talk about professionalism from the other night. He honestly had no idea what he'd been saying. He had dated a fellow chef back in Paris, and she had ruined his entire pot of Bolognese. But Nikki wasn't anything like Claire, and Paul really thought he could date someone he worked with.

The truth was, he'd been dating his career for the past five years, trying to be the best he could be at Holly Hanson's. He hadn't even realized how much more sat beyond the door of a restaurant until Nikki had walked through it.

He took a deep breath and reminded himself that she was not his girlfriend. Just because they got along great and he found her attractive didn't mean they were anything more than partners doing a three-day pop-up restaurant.

After that ended, he'd need to find another job or figure out what to do to start his own restaurant.

He knocked on the door, and Angela pulled it open only a second later. "Oh," she said, stumbling back. "Go on up. She's in the kitchen." Angela ducked out, leaving Paul to face the steps alone.

Nikki was indeed sitting at the kitchen table, several sheets of paper spread in front of her. Her apartment was an embodiment of her in things. Vintage toasters. Hand-painted salt shakers. Bleached wood furniture. His gaze lingered on the framed menus on the wall, but he was drawn to Nikki, who wore a vibrant red sweater and a joyful smile.

He sat at the table and leaned over the notebook she'd been writing in. "This menu is perfect, but I think we should supplement my recipes with a few more dishes."

"What were you thinking?"

"How about your heart-shaped ravioli?"

Paul made a face and looked away. Holly's evaluation of his dish ran through his mind. "You don't think that was too tacky?"

"I think it's romantic."

Paul ducked his head and grinned, more happiness skipping through him than he'd ever experienced, even when he'd landed in Paris and started at the prestigious Le Cordon Bleu culinary arts institute.

They spent the day getting food orders put in and buying the rest of the supplies they needed. Back at Gus's Kitchen, they pulled tables and chairs into the configuration Nikki wanted. Paul climbed the ladder and hung the highest hearts while Jerrod and Angela unpacked glasses and plates, and Nikki designed menus.

By the end of the evening, the Kitchen had been transformed into something even the ritziest couples would love to be caught eating in. He glanced around after Nikki had stepped onto the sidewalk.

"You coming?" she asked, and her voice sent sweetness straight through him.

"Coming."

She practically skipped down the street, the lights causing a glow to halo her head, and he grinned as she talked about all they'd accomplished in just a few short days.

"We're meeting with Angela tomorrow," she said when they reached her apartment, and Paul paused. Did he walk her to the door? It was only up six steps. He tucked his hands into his pockets.

"What time?" he asked, his voice catching in his throat for some reason. Maybe because he really wanted to kiss Nikki goodnight.

"Ten okay?"

"Ten's great."

She lowered her head in her shy-sexy way and went up the steps. Paul watched her, and she glanced back at him, a flirty smile already gracing her mouth. He waved and she went inside, closing the door between them.

Paul continued down the street toward his apartment. His phone rang and he picked up the call from the restaurant supply store.

"We have the jacket in white," Hazel confirmed. "You said a female small?"

Paul closed his eyes and tipped his head back to the stars. He hoped he could guess Nikki's size appropriately. "Yes," he said. "Female small. And you can do the embroidery by Wednesday?"

The pop-up shop opened Thursday night for

Valentine's Day, and he really wanted Nikki to be wearing a chef's jacket all three days. She deserved it.

"I can," Hazel said. "Let me just confirm...let's see...oh, here it is. You wanted Nikki, spelled N-I-K-K-I on the left side, done in a rosy pink. Is that right?"

"That's right," Paul said.

"I'll call you when it's ready," she said. "Shouldn't be past tomorrow."

"Thanks." Paul hung up and continued home, his step a little lighter. He was amazed at how much he and Nikki had been able to accomplish in just a few days. Having Jerrod and Angela's help had really boosted their productivity, and Paul thought about getting a thank you gift for his friends, too.

His friends.

He smiled to himself as he walked. He finally had people he could consider real friends—and it felt good.

Angela bustled around the apartment in her bare feet, clearly not ready for their ten a.m. meeting. Paul didn't mind. Since he wouldn't be working until midnight—or later—behind the stove, he didn't need to sleep in as much.

He stood in front of Nikki's framed menus as she explained what they were. She finished and looked up at him, another moment crystallizing between them. His fingers twitched toward hers, but Angela said, "All right. I'm ready."

Nikki looked away first, breaking the spell, and went to sit beside Angela at the refinished kitchen table. Paul joined them, sandwiching Angela between them so they could both see the laptop screen in front of her.

"So we're all set to post to Facebook, Twitter, Tumblr, The Patch, Reddit. I've got a friend at the *Tribune* who's gonna blog about it. And I've got some of the city's top food critics coming in. They were scheduled to go to Holly Hanson's for a tasting, but I convinced them that this was an extravaganza they didn't want to miss." She glanced at Nikki and Paul, a satisfied look on her face.

Nikki emitted her cute little giggle and bumped Angela with her shoulder.

Paul was impressed. He hadn't spent much time on social media and barely knew who the food critics in the city were. Holly had handled all of that—or rather, her assistant usually had.

"All I need is a name," Angela said, glancing first at Nikki and then at Paul. "What are you guys gonna call it?"

Paul hadn't even thought about titling the pop-up. He raised his eyebrows and looked at Nikki. "How about…Nikki and Paul's?"

"Paul and Nikki's?" she suggested.

He half-shrugged, half-cringed. "That's not much better."

"Hmm…" Nikki looked up, like the ceiling might

hold some answers to what they should call their Valentine's Day pop-up.

"How about Two Hearts Pop-up?" Angela suggested, but Nikki made a face like she'd smelled something bad.

"I Love You Pop-up?" Angela tried next, but Paul moaned his disagreement.

Nikki started musing, saying, "Valentine's Day… Valentine's Day…"

Paul's mind circled the themes of Valentine's Day and what it all meant. Commitment. Romance. Love.

He realized Holly had been wrong when it came to flowers and hearts being décor. They were Valentine's Day. What else embodied the holiday?

"What about Café Cupid?" he suggested. He waved his hand and looked at Nikki.

She smiled, her Valentine's Day-colored lips spreading into a beautiful smile. "Yeah, that's perfect."

"Café Cupid it is." Angela started typing, and later that day, Paul and Nikki stopped by the print shop to pick up the simply designed sign for their pop-up shop.

Light pink with a darker pink heart with Cupid's arrow and the same rosy pink for the lettering that he'd chosen for Nikki's chef's jacket, the sign fit nicely in the window. Nikki changed the letters below it to "2 more days!" and turned to beam at him.

Paul felt the strength of their friendship grow, and he once again wondered if it could be more. He returned to the task of sending the menus out to be printed, the last thing he needed to accomplish that day, leaving his thoughts for another time when there wasn't so much to do.

Chapter Sixteen

Paul left for Café Cupid earlier than he needed to because he had one stop to make before he went in. Well, two, actually.

The first was at the restaurant clothing supply store, where he picked up Nikki's chef's jacket from Hazel, the woman that had been supplying Holly for years. She was petite and stout, and Paul had to almost bend in half to hug her.

"This is amazing," he said, holding up the jacket. "I think it's going to fit great."

"Let me know if it doesn't," Hazel said. "I can tailor it." She watched Paul with a motherly eye, but he didn't offer any further explanation, didn't tell her who Nikki was. He paid for the jacket and went to the stationery and party supply store where they'd bought the decorations for the pop-up. He wasn't after huge sheets of paper he could mold into hearts this time, but a gift bag and a card for his pop-up partner.

He labored over the card but only ended up with a few words. So he wasn't Nikki, who had the gift of gab and could really give someone a thoughtful compliment. Though his note was short, every word meant something to him, and he carefully folded the jacket and placed it in the bottom of the bag, layering pink tissue paper over it and sticking the card down the side.

He didn't even care that he was carrying a very pink bag down the streets of Lakeside. He arrived at Café Cupid before Nikki, thankfully, and stashed the gift bag under the front register, where he hoped an appropriate time to present it to her would arise naturally.

She'd clearly been there, because fresh flowers and precisely placed ribbons sat on the bar where patrons would usually eat bacon and eggs. But Nikki had wanted this to feel more intimate, and she wasn't using the bar for more than decoration.

He went back into the kitchen to make sure they had the ingredients and kitchen items they needed. Someone banged on the back door, and he opened it to find the restaurant supply company with the tablecloths they'd ordered.

"Right here," he said as the guy started bringing them in.

Out front, a phone rang, and he heard Nikki's voice. His heartbeat banged against his ribs, and he forced himself to walk slowly out to greet her.

She hung up as he approached and twisted toward him, a hugely excited look on her face. "We just sold out!"

Her enthusiasm was contagious.

"Sold out?" he asked.

"Yeah, we're completely booked for all three nights!" She laughed, and the relief and happiness pouring through him sent a chuckle out of his mouth, too. He engulfed her in a hug and held on.

He wanted to pause time, really keep her in his arms for a while and see if she'd stay. She certainly wasn't pulling away, and Paul's heart swelled as his eyes closed in bliss.

Then he remembered everything she'd said about her ex-boyfriend.

But you're not him, he thought. And you do support her dreams.

He pulled back slightly, moving slow and stopping when he was only inches from her face. He looked at her eyes, but she was already focused on his mouth.

She lifted her gaze to his, and he saw the same desire in her expression that he felt swirling in his gut.

His voice said, "Sorry, this is…"

She patted his chest and seemed more sure of herself when she said, "Not a good idea."

"And very unprofessional." Would she contradict him? Why was he even saying that?

"Unprofessional." She swallowed hard. "Yes. Don't want another cayenne pepper incident." She slipped her hands from his shoulders, where they'd fit so naturally, and stepped back as far as the counter would let her.

He nodded and smiled, because he couldn't really speak at the moment.

"Nikki!" Angela's voice came from the kitchen, and Nikki startled in that direction.

"I think I hear Angela calling me." She giggled nervously and stumbled, putting a few more feet between them.

"Yeah. Yeah, and I've got some work." He pointed to a vase of flowers, his mind still reeling from the soft rain scent of her hair and the way she'd rubbed his shoulders during their embrace.

She walked toward the back, and he finally ironed out his thoughts long enough to remember the chef's jacket. "Nikki!" he called after her.

He bent to retrieve the bag, holding it in front of him like a shield as she retraced her steps back to him, a sweet smile on her face. "For opening night." He handed her the gift.

She received his present with reverence, setting the bag down and plucking the card from the tissue paper first. "To Nikki, otherwise known as Chef." She looked up at him with such adoration, he had to believe she felt the same things between them as he did.

"Love, Paul. Wow."

He folded his arms and watched as she lifted the jacket out and gazed at it with wonder. He liked making her feel good about herself, liked the shy look she gave him when she said, "Thanks. I love it."

She left the bag but took the card and the jacket with her as she went to find her friend. Paul felt warm from head to toe and exhaled a breath he hadn't realized he'd been holding.

Chapter Seventeen

"**I** thought you said you had time to go shopping today," Angela said in the kitchen.

"I do." Nikki traced her fingertip along the rosy pink threads in her name, her thoughts far from this conversation.

"Well, come on then." Angela gently took the chef's jacket from Nikki and set it on the clean prep table. "You'll have to tell me all about what's got you all dazed," she said in her best friend voice. "And I'm guessing it has something to do with that jacket."

Nikki's vocal chords felt all plugged up. Frozen or something.

Paul was very nice. She'd been so busy she hadn't even thought about a gift for him, and he'd gone ahead and given her the greatest thing. The *only* thing she'd ever wanted.

Angela towed her out of the kitchen and into the weak February sunlight. That seemed to thaw Nikki's inability to speak, because she told Angela all about how they'd booked every seat in the café for all three nights, then all about the wonderful moment—or maybe a whole bunch of moments—she'd shared with Paul.

She ended with the chef's jacket right as they pushed their way into Nikki's favorite boutique. She didn't have a lot of money, but she did want to wear something special for opening night. As she stepped over to a rack of dresses, Angela asked, "So you almost kissed?"

"Well, almost." She flipped through the clothes, searching for something that would look good with the jacket. Maybe something black… "Then it kind of turned into an awkward hug."

"What are you going to do about it?"

"Do about it? There's nothing to do about it." She glanced over to where Angela was digging through another rack. "Okay? Paul and I have a professional relationship."

"Oh, I don't buy that for a minute." Angela always did say things how they were. "You gotta let your walls down, Nikki. I mean, give the guy a shot."

Nikki really wanted to give him a shot. More than one. But his story about the cayenne pepper Bolognese had been on a loop inside her brain for days. He'd seemed so serious about keeping things professional, and even just a few minutes ago, he could've kissed her, but he didn't.

"I just—I don't think we should cross that line," Nikki said. "It's unprofessional."

"Oh, now you just sound like Holly." If Angela had wanted to twist the knife into Nikki's chest, she certainly knew how. "Lots of people who work together fall in love."

Nikki abandoned the dress rack and turned toward Angela, surprise written all over her face. "Love?"

"Look, you're only human, Nikki. As much as you don't want to, it is inevitable that you will fall in love again. He's probably falling for you, too." Angela smiled like that was a good thing, but Nikki wasn't so sure. She'd felt the strength in Paul's arms, felt safe and warm in his embrace. She'd seen the heat in his gaze only minutes ago, and yet, he'd done nothing.

She left the dress rack and walked toward Angela. "Look, I…I appreciate your optimism, Ang. I do. But you and I both know…I'm just not really relationship material." The words hurt coming out, but they were absolutely true. Ever since Ryan, she hadn't been able to start something serious with another man, almost like she'd constructed a wall between her and everyone who might be interested. Paul hadn't seemed to have any problem getting around it, but Nikki thought it was only a matter of time. "So. Let's just drop this."

Angela wore a look of sympathy, agreed, and went back to the racks. Nikki did, too, no longer really in the mood for dress shopping, if that was even possible.

"What do you think about this one?" She pulled a black dress from the rack without checking the size.

"Too plain. This is your big night. You gotta make a statement." Angela reached for a dress and held it up. All blue lace, the dress was off-the-charts outrageous and had no place inside a kitchen. "Now, this is what I'm talking about."

Nikki eyed it, trying to decide what she'd rather wear for her big night. "Okay." She took the dress and went to try it on. While she shimmied into the garment, she couldn't help wondering what Paul would think of it. How would he react to it?

The dress fit well, and she slid her palms down her sides and over her hips. It didn't matter what Paul thought about the dress, not if they were strictly professional. She cocked her head at her reflection, wondering if she should talk to him about taking things along a more personal track.

For tonight, she told herself, you're friends and business partners. Not dating.

So she wouldn't buy this dress in the hopes that he would like it or to draw a particular reaction from him.

She'd buy it because it fit well, she liked how feminine and fun it made her feel, and because she deserved it. She'd buy it for herself. A treat for the past four days of hard work. For all the preparation she'd put into Café Cupid.

And if Paul happened to like the dress, that was just an added bonus.

With Angela on the way back to the apartment with the dress, Nikki turned into Delucci's to place another order for the following day. She hoped Trish and Marty would have time to fulfill the dozens and dozens of rolls Nikki needed to make the peanut butter root beer beef stew an instant hit.

She found them both at the counter as it was almost closing time for the bakery, and she slid them a piece of paper with what she needed. "I'm so sorry for the last-minute order, but it's just—well, we kind of threw everything together. I mean, we only finalized the menu last night. But I guess that's why they call it a pop-up restaurant." She giggled, realizing once again that she'd started babbling. She paused and wondered, Why am I nervous?

She knew the answer. Paul. After all, these were Paul's parents. And she already knew they weren't coming to Café Cupid on any of the three nights. She'd wanted to tell Paul to invite his parents. She'd save a table for them. But he'd asked her to let him deal with his family, and Nikki wanted to respect that.

"Of course we can fill the order." Trish leaned forward and chuckled.

"Where is it gonna be again?" Marty asked as he wrote on a custom order form.

"At Gus's Kitchen, downtown. Yeah, he's going to rent us out the space."

"Us?" Marty looked up, right at her face. "You have a partner?"

Nikki's smile fell at the same rate her heart plummeted. So Paul hadn't said anything. Not even that he was helping her. Nothing. What was she supposed to do? Lie?

"Well, yes. It's…Paul." She glanced at Trish, hoping to get some support. She got a blank stare in return.

"Paul?" The level of surprise in Marty's voice wasn't exactly comforting. "My Paul is gonna be your cooking partner?"

"Well, it's mainly going to be my recipes, but we are featuring a few of his originals, as well."

"Originals?" Again with the awed tone. His voice squirmed through Nikki's ears in an uncomfortable way. "Sounds fancy. Sounds like Paul. Big chef and too good to be a baker." Marty walked away, and Nikki's heart screamed at her to get him to come back.

But Paul had expressly asked her to stay out of the Delucci family feud. She looked at Trish, who wore a look halfway between hopeful and hurt. Nikki couldn't stand seeing her like that and remembered how Paul had said Trish had gotten caught in the middle of all of this.

She opened her mouth, sure it was about to get her in trouble. "No. You should come," she blurted.

Thankfully, Marty turned back. "To the opening?"

Trish gasped and said, "How wonderful would that be?" She clearly wanted to attend, and Nikki could tell she just wanted Paul and Marty to reconcile everything between them.

"No," Marty said.

"Oh, come on, Marty." She laughed, but the tension between them was palpable, and Nikki felt like an intruder on their private family matter—doing exactly what Paul had asked her not to do.

"What?" Marty asked. "What do you want me to say?" He turned to Nikki. "Listen, I just know Paul really wouldn't want me there."

"Oh, no. You're wrong. He would love it if you were there. It would mean so much to him. And for you to try one of his recipes..." Couldn't Marty see that was all Paul wanted?

"He's making a ravioli that's just out of this world," she ended, not quite sure what else to say to get Marty to come. If she should even be inviting him at all.

"If my son wanted me there, he would send an invitation."

"Listen, just consider this an invitation, okay?" Nikki said. "From me."

He sighed heavily. "I'll consider it." But he didn't look like he was really thinking about coming at all. He glanced at Trish, and so did Nikki. "Okay."

Trish looked so hopeful, but Nikki didn't want Marty to feel like they were ganging up on him, so she glanced down and nodded before thanking them and heading back outside. She changed her mind with every step she took.

Inviting them was a good thing—the right thing—to do.

You should've stayed out of their business.

All Paul wants is for his father to taste one of his recipes. This way, he will.

If he even comes. What will you do if he doesn't come? What will you do if he does?

Nikki banished the voices, the doubts, all of it as she arrived back at Café Cupid. Her heart pumped out a few extra beats as she opened the door and caught a glimpse of Paul's broad shoulders through the window. He stirred something, a thoughtful look on his face, and Nikki remembered all the times she'd stood in that kitchen cooking.

She drew in a deep breath. This was her restaurant for the next three days, and she was going to make sure everyone in Lakeside knew she'd been here—even if Marty and Trish didn't come.

Paul looked up and caught her eye, a smile filling his handsome face. He gestured for her to join him, that he had something he wanted to show her, and she once again thought that she should've brought him a present after the way he'd tailor-made that chef's jacket for her.

If his parents come, she thought. *That will be gift enough.* Giddiness bubbled through her as she shrugged out of her coat and stepped over to try Paul's Alfredo sauce.

Paul picked up a towel and wiped the counter. Everything had been prepped. He'd spent most of the day with Nikki already, the scent of her perfume permeating his senses until he thought he'd go mad.

He really wanted to enjoy a Valentine's Day meal with her—and he would. They'd started their pop-up right on Valentine's Day. Now he just needed to work up the nerve to ask her to join him for dinner.

Tonight.

She didn't have great memories of Valentine's Day, and he'd love to change that for her. Be the man who wined her and dined her and held her hand as he walked her home. He wanted to cook with her, collaborate with her, kiss her goodnight.

Careful. You're thinking way ahead of where you actually are.

He knew he was. But as Nikki emerged from the back room wearing a lacy blue dress under her chef's jacket, a flash of a future with her stole through Paul. And he didn't care if he was thinking too far ahead.

The embrace earlier may have been premature. Or maybe it had been exactly what she needed to see that he wanted more than "professional" with her. He'd kicked himself a thousand times since those blasted words had come out of his mouth.

Very unprofessional.

What a very unprofessional thing to say to someone he certainly wanted to become very personal with.

"So what do you think?" Nikki did a little twirl for him that left his throat too narrow.

"Uh, looks great." He gave her a smile he hoped would smooth over the rough edges in his voice. She was the most beautiful woman he'd ever met. She'd twisted her hair back differently tonight and done something with her makeup that made her eyes seem larger and more mysterious. She was mature, kind, talented, and the attraction he felt toward her ratcheted up another notch.

His fingers twitched toward her, and he snatched up a wooden spoon and stirred his Alfredo sauce so he wouldn't lunge for her and hold her against his chest again.

Excitement dove through him at the thought of eating dinner with her, and he had to ask her soon.

"Nikki—"

"We're open!" She squealed as Angela opened the door and their first guests stepped inside. Paul watched Nikki, who gazed into the dining room with wonder and happiness on her face.

Everything inside him softened. She'd wanted to open a restaurant her whole life, and now her dream was coming true. He was glad he could play a small part in it, and the tricky little thought of expanding this enterprise beyond the three days snuck into his mind.

Would she go for it? He had some savings; he could financially back them until they got things going. With something else to talk to her about, he felt stuffed full of words with no time to say them.

The dining room filled with chatter as every table got taken. Waiters and waitresses scurried from couple to couple, Jerrod poured wine, and before Paul knew it, the first orders appeared in the window.

Nikki took a deep breath and met his eyes with more excitement in hers than he'd seen anyone wear in a long time. "Let's do this," she said.

He smiled and nodded, a touch of her enthusiasm rubbing off on him. After all, tonight wasn't the same old job of cooking someone else's recipes. Tonight, he'd be serving his own creations.

A blip of uncertainty shot through him, especially when he saw four orders of his heart-shaped ravioli on the first few tickets.

Then he rolled up his proverbial sleeves and got to work.

He and Nikki perfected their dance in the small kitchen in about five minutes. She worked the waffle fried chicken and peanut butter root beer beef stew while he took care of all the appetizers and his ravioli.

He could anticipate her every move, and she seemed to be able to do the same. Paul had never felt so much heat while working in a kitchen before, and Nikki kept shooting him quick glances. He hoped she felt the same level of…whatever this was between them.

"Truffle oil?" he asked as she prepared to put another plate of lamb chops in the window.

"Yep. Could you pass me the—"

He handed her the bottle of raspberry sauce before she could even identify it. A surge of satisfaction soared through him at her happy sigh. She took the sauce and plated her food expertly.

Paul turned away from her, a dangerous smile riding his mouth. "I gotta admit, this is the most fun that I've ever had in the kitchen." There. He'd said it.

"Yeah, I know. This is how it's supposed to be, right?" She continued working, obviously unaware of the emotion in his voice.

He glanced at her and forged on. "It's all thanks to you. You made this happen."

"No, *we* did." A smile filled her face and her voice. "We're a team now."

We. He liked the sound of that. He liked it a lot. "So maybe we should start thinking beyond the next three days." He paused in his work and leaned onto the corner of the counter to focus on her. "Like maybe something permanent."

That got her attention, and she swung those beautiful eyes toward him. They were wide and filled with questions. "Permanent?"

"Yeah, like a permanent space." He gestured to the diner beyond the window. It was great and all, but not exactly the kind of restaurant he wanted to build for the two of them.

Her face fell for half a heartbeat before she covered the emotion with a grin and turned back to her plates. "A restaurant space. Right."

"Too presumptuous?" Paul tilted his head to see her better. She swung back toward him, and he decided to lay all his cards on the table. Well, maybe not all of them. "I mean, you do want to do this with me, right?"

"Yes, of course I do! Absolutely."

He chuckled nervously and nodded.

"Yeah," she said, getting back to work. There was something off, something...nervous or hesitant in her that he couldn't put his finger on. No matter what it was, he didn't like it.

Before he could ask her about it, Angela bustled into the kitchen, pure joy etched into her features. "You guys have got to come and see this!" She waved at both of them to follow her. Paul put down his towel and went with Nikki into the dining room.

The place looked like Cupid himself had shown up and decorated with glitter and flowers in shades of pink, white, red, and lots of purple. Their paper decorations didn't look so cheesy with the addition of the fresh floral arrangements, and the low lighting cast romantic shadows on everything.

Angela stopped just outside the kitchen and waited for Nikki and Paul to join her. "You know you've made it when your customers are posting photos of their meals on social media."

Paul tore his eyes from the décor to focus on the actual patrons. A woman in a slinky black dress had her phone out, snapping a picture of his ravioli. *His* ravioli.

A couple at the bar zoomed in on a plate of Nikki's waffle fried chicken, the man clicked to take a picture, and Paul heard the woman say, "Put that on Instagram. No filter."

A sense of wonder infiltrated Paul's thoughts. He'd been working in a professional kitchen for years, and he'd never experienced this level of excitement before. He'd loved being Holly's executive chef, and the loss of that job had hit him hard. But now... Now none of that mattered. Now he knew that he wanted to create his own recipes, serve his own food, taste this kind of anticipation and awe every time he experimented with a new pork dish or invented a new soup recipe.

Beside him, Nikki couldn't stop smiling.

"Congratulations! You're a hit!" Angela said. She pointed to the corner, where a man in a dark suit sat in a booth. "Not to mention, you have the top food critic in the city here!" He smiled at his dining partners and wrote something in an open notebook at his side.

"You're gonna get your name and your recipes out before Holly," Angela said, sending an arrow of hope right through Paul's heart. He wanted Nikki to get the credit she deserved, wanted her to be happy more than anything.

"Wow." He was unsure if his feelings for Nikki

made this a wow-moment—or maybe it was because everything had come together perfectly for this pop-up. Perhaps it was both.

"Wow," Nikki repeated. She looked back to Paul, but he didn't know what else to say. She drew in a deep breath, and it sounded hard for her to do. "Um, can you guys just...give me a minute?" She stepped back into the kitchen, but Paul didn't want to leave the vibrant atmosphere of the café.

"That's great." He smiled at Angela and gazed out to the crowd one more time. Additional people waited for their reservation, and the urge to get back to work pulled through Paul. He returned to the kitchen, too, but Nikki wasn't there.

Concern tugged at his heart, and he caught sight of the open door in the back. He strode that way, leaving the orders for a few minutes.

She stood in the alley, her breath steaming in front of her as she exhaled. Someone had adorned the outside of the café with yellow and pink tea lights and a red paper lantern, casting rosy streaks onto her hair.

"Nikki?" He paused in the doorway, wanting to give her the space she'd requested, yet desperate to go to her at the same time. "You okay?"

She turned toward him, her face radiant and alive. "Yeah. Yeah. I just, uh. I just..."

He approached, removing his apron, too, the way she had. He tucked his hands into his pockets as she continued.

"I don't know, I got really overwhelmed in there. You know? I mean, I'm living my dream right now... at this very moment, and...it's surreal." She looked at him with a level of vulnerability he'd never seen her wear. She'd shared some of the deepest parts of herself with him, and he wasn't going to waste those.

Music from the restaurant filtered through the door and lifted into the air around them. "I love this song."

Paul forgot all about cooking. He put out his hand. "May I?"

"Are you kidding?" She trilled out a little giggle.

"You don't think I know how to dance?" He infused a level of playfulness into his tone that completely obscured the jittery feeling in his stomach. He wanted to touch her so badly.

"No, I'm just saying, one of us should, uh..." She laughed. "Be in the kitchen. You know?"

"We've got an experienced staff from one of the best restaurants in the city. I think they'll be able to manage for a few minutes." He drew her into his arms, and she came willingly, a fact that didn't escape his attention.

His muscles sighed at the contact between them, relieved to have her in his embrace once more. He realized as they matched their rhythm to the music that she belonged there, and he couldn't tear his gaze from hers.

She couldn't seem to look away, either. "Ah, so romantic."

Paul took a deep breath and tried to organize his words. They refused to line up, so he just opened his mouth and let himself speak. "You know, it's not just cooking with you that I enjoy." There was no smile. No nervous chuckle. Just her and him. Just her hand in his, and her body moving in time with his.

"This is nice, too." He half-sighed as she continued to gaze at him. He could usually read everything she was thinking, but tonight, under these weak lights, he was struggling to see how she felt about him. He dropped his head for a fraction of a moment.

He looked back at her, now ready to get his own emotions out in the open. "I was wondering if maybe you'd like to join me for dinner when we finish tonight?"

Her face split into a smile. "Like a Valentine's Day dinner?"

"Yeah, like a Valentine's Day dinner."

"Okay, sure." She nodded. "I'd like that."

He edged closer, drawing her tighter against him. His eyes dropped to her mouth, his fantasies about kissing her later ballooning through his mind. She leaned into his touch, and he skated his lips across her temple, closing his eyes in bliss. He hadn't felt this way about anyone in a long time. In fact, the last time he'd felt this strongly about something, it was culinary school, not a woman.

Her hand held his and pressed right against his heart as they continued to sway to the music. Paul took a breath and made a conscious effort to commit this moment to memory so he'd never have to live without it.

It felt like time had slowed and accelerated at the same time, and then Angela said, "There you are," causing Nikki to lean away from him, though she didn't remove her hand from his shoulder.

"One of you needs to get out front and schmooze." Angela left as fast as she'd come, no judgment or surprise on her face.

Nikki slid her hand down his bicep, sending a thrill all the way to the top of his head. "You go," she said.

He didn't want to leave her, but he backed away slowly, the absence of her touch almost painful. He smiled as he turned and went back into the kitchen and then out to the dining room, everything whirling inside him as that romantic song continued to fill his ears.

Chapter Eighteen

Holly adjusted the plate she'd laid on the bar an eighth of an inch, as if that made a difference. Darkness had fallen an hour ago, and the food was ready in the back. She'd personally prepared the waffle fried chicken herself. Being in her own kitchen again had been exhilarating yet terrifying. Maybe if she spent more time in front of the stove, she'd rediscover some inspiration for creating recipes.

But she'd been pulled from the kitchen by constant texts about the remodel, a call from the food supplier, and several questions from her assistant. All of those things reminded her that she was more than a chef now. That she simply didn't have time to exercise her creative muscles. Not when there was an entire empire to manage.

With the plate in place, all she needed was the critics to arrive. She checked her watch and then the front door. They were late. Fifteen minutes late.

It wasn't like any of them to be tardy. Usually, they showed up early, trying to catch her unprepared.

Her new assistant, Jayda, approached. "Where on earth is everybody? I thought you had critics lined up to come sample." Holly touched the bar but kept her gaze lasered at this new woman. She wasn't anywhere near as good as Nikki, and the loss of the late-night cooking show had also been a real blow for Holly.

Jayda at least had the decency to look concerned. "That's what I was coming to tell you. They canceled."

"They canceled? All of them?"

Jayda nodded, a nervous edge entering her eye. "Yes, all of them. I looked up online, and I think they're going to that big pop-up event downtown."

Holly had no idea what the girl was saying. "Pop-up?"

"This new chef, Nikki Turner," Jayda started, and Holly winced, hoping it just looked like a blink. First off, Nikki wasn't a chef.

"She's doing this cool three-night thing called Café Cupid," Jayda finished.

Pure fear flowed through Holly. She cleared her throat so it wouldn't show in her voice when she asked, "The address?"

She had to get over there and see what Nikki was serving. As Jayda scribbled some numbers for somewhere right downtown—a perfect hot spot for Valentine's Day—Holly had a sick feeling in her stomach that she knew what would be on the menu.

How could she stop Nikki from ruining her?

Holly pushed away the insecurities that had been let out of the box she kept them in with just two simple words. Pop-up.

No matter what, she'd do what she had to do to maintain her reputation.

Paul knew the moment Nikki had returned to the kitchen because he could feel her eyes tracking him as he went through the dining room, asking the guests about their entrees.

He went to the window, grabbed a plate of food for a table, and took it to them, his smile hitched in place. At least until his eyes fell on a couple sitting in a booth several paces away.

He knew that silver hair, those honey-blonde curls. His father's eyes were closed, the lines between them obvious as he frowned.

Paul's insides froze, and all the noise from the other diners fell into silence.

He must've drifted close enough to them because his mother spotted him, her face breaking into a gushing smile. "Sweetheart, it is fabulous!"

He stepped over to their table, though every cell in his body urged him to turn around and run. "Mom. Dad. What are you guys doing here?"

"What kind of a welcome is that? Huh?" his father asked.

Of course, Paul had done that wrong, too. Nothing he did was ever right in his father's eyes. "I mean, I'm—I'm surprised to see you, is all."

"Nikki invited us."

His father might as well have stabbed him with those three words. "Nikki?"

"Nikki, yeah."

Paul turned back to the kitchen, but a waiter obstructed his view of Nikki. "Well, I sure didn't receive an invite from you, now did I?" His dad had perfected the dose of disappointment in his voice over the years.

His mom tried to cover the awkwardness with her usual level of bubbliness. "She just told us some of your recipes were going to be featured."

He had no idea how to feel. Anger clashed with hope, which warred with disappointment. He didn't want to hear his father's critique of his food, couldn't believe Nikki had invited them, couldn't shoulder the well of anticipation in his mother's eyes.

"I gotta go." He thumbed the air behind him, confusion taking front and center in his brain. "I gotta get back to the kitchen. We're...really busy."

"Paul, wait, I—I—"

He was vaguely aware of his father calling to him, but Paul couldn't turn. That half-eaten plate of heart-shaped ravioli on the table in front of his dad burned the back of his eyelids. Paul saw it every time he blinked, and he just...couldn't. Not tonight.

Nikki handled the orders just fine without Paul. The vibe wasn't the same in the small space when she was alone, though, and every nerve ending in her body testified to it. He shared the burden of expectation, and she'd appreciated it. Plus, putting together a plate of his pasta without him felt wrong almost.

Still, she put up order after order, her heart thundering when Paul came over and took a plate, flashing her a quick smile before he returned to the floor. A few minutes later, he stepped back into the kitchen, his face screwed up in concentration—or frustration. Nikki couldn't exactly pinpoint it. He stood with his back to her, not really doing anything.

"Everything okay out there?" she asked, the tension between them suddenly very awkward and charged.

Paul barely moved. "Everything's fine." He spun around and shook something on the stove, sending it into a sizzle.

Nikki put up a plate and shot a glance at him out of the corner of her eye. He was definitely not fine, even if things in the dining room were humming along. "You sure you're okay?"

After wiping a plate, he put it up in the window. He leaned against the counter, his face broadcasting his distress. "My dad is out there." He met her eye with a challenge in his.

Nikki's stomach swooped, but it was nothing like what had happened in the alley when Paul had taken her hand in his and tucked her against his body.

"He says that you invited him," he said. "Why would you do that?"

She glanced toward the dining room, as if someone would be able to help her. But she felt very much alone. "Oh… Well, I—I stopped at the bakery yesterday, and I…"

He turned his back as soon as she said the word "bakery," and Nikki's voice trailed off at the end.

Paul worked, spun back to her, and enunciated his words with his hands. "What? You thought that you'd just invite him? Without asking me?"

Nikki hadn't thought about it like that. "Well, yes. I suppose I did." When she was at the bakery, she didn't feel like she could lie to Marty about who her partner was. She hadn't done it maliciously—though she had known Paul wouldn't be happy about it.

Hadn't she?

Hadn't she argued with herself about this very thing?

"I asked you specifically to not get involved." He barely looked at her when he spoke, and that cut deeper than the actual words themselves.

Panic poured through her, and her voice reflected it when she said, "I wasn't trying to get involved. I just—"

"You just—" Paul cut her off, obviously

disinterested in what she had to say. Her heart hurt when he put his head in his hand. "You shouldn't have done that. Everything was going so well tonight." He peered out the service window. "I wasn't expecting to deal with my judgmental father tasting my food for the first time." He went back to work, the conversation clearly closed.

Nikki felt like a fool. She hadn't realized the emotional preparation he'd need to do in order to have Marty eat his food. She hadn't realized that Paul expected his father to criticize his food, not praise it. She hadn't realized a lot of things, and her chest squeezed.

But there were orders that needed filling and another wave of reservations still to go. They danced in the kitchen, putting up beautiful plates of delicious food, but it wasn't the same as when they'd started. He didn't hand her the raspberry sauce or ask if he could dot on the truffle oil.

And it was nothing like the heart-throbbing, romantic dance she'd shared with him in the alleyway. Their eyes met again and again, and each time, he exhaled like he had something to say but it wasn't worth the effort.

Nikki couldn't find the right words to apologize for what she'd done, and their work in the kitchen ended when a waiter picked up the last two plates and Angela announced, "That's it! Last order has officially gone out."

Nikki chuckled, unsure as to why. Maybe she just wanted to paint over her exhaustion as well as the foolishness still racing through her.

"So, you can take it from here?" Paul asked.

She whipped toward him to find him leaning against that counter again, so sexy and yet so closed off. "Oh, you want to leave?" He'd asked her to stay for dinner not two hours ago. As she looked into his clouded eyes, the possibility of sharing a romantic meal with him, the scent of candlelight and roses as companions, faded to a distant dot on the horizon.

He exhaled again. "Yeah." At least he had the guts to look right into her eyes when he said, "I'll see you tomorrow."

Horror was the only thing she could feel, the only thing her body could convey, the only note in her voice when she said, "Okay."

He actually looked to Angela. "Great work tonight." He turned and left the kitchen, untying his apron as he went, never once looking back.

Great work tonight?

To Angela?

Nikki glanced down at the impeccably clean counter where she'd worked all night, then back to the stove where all her dishes had come together in layers of flavors and textures. She'd done a great job tonight.

And so had he.

They were so good together, both professionally and—Nikki had hoped—personally.

"What just happened?" Angela asked.

What happened was that she hadn't apologized. Hadn't even explained why she'd thought having his father there was a good idea. Because maybe it wasn't.

"Well, I, uh…" Nikki barely knew where to start. "Earlier, I, uh…"

Beth, who'd been acting as their hostess for the evening, appeared, her face in a bit of a twist. "Nikki, I need you to come out front right away. It's urgent."

Though Nikki felt tired from head to toe and front to back, she followed Beth, who led her to the booth where the food critic had been sitting.

Nikki froze—every part of her except her heart—when she saw the long, dark locks of Holly Hanson. She stood with her back to Nikki, but the words were said loud enough to carry to every remaining customer in Café Cupid.

"Nikki Turner stole my recipes," Holly said.

Nikki sucked in a breath, the exact scenario she'd wanted to avoid playing out in front of her, live and in color.

"Really?" At least the food critic sounded dubious.

"She was my assistant, and I fired her," Holly said with passion. "She must've invited you to get some press. To pretend that these are her new recipes. Isn't that a shame? For someone to stoop so low? To steal from someone?"

Nikki could barely breathe. The food critic looked

at Nikki, still unmoving as if the floor had caged her feet in an invisible trap.

Holly turned, too, but she spun back to the critic before Nikki could truly look at her. Everything seemed fuzzy around the edges, and Nikki wanted nothing more than to go home and forget this night had ever happened.

No. Tonight had been wonderful. All of her dreams coming true—at least her professional dreams of owning her own restaurant, serving her food to the people of Lakeside, and making a name for herself.

And there was Holly Hanson, trying to ruin that name before it had even settled in people's brains.

"So, please," Holly said. "This menu will be featured at my new restaurant when I open after my renovations are completed. I hope you'll come and be my personal guest." She extended her hand for the critic to shake.

He did, and added, "I'll be there." His gaze landed on Nikki again, and it felt like he'd already judged her. His critique of her food was already done. He'd already believed Holly.

"Thank you." Holly turned and took the few steps to Nikki, who squared her shoulders and refused to look away. Still, her insides felt like someone had encased them in gelatin, because they shook and shimmied as she waited for Holly to say something. To tell the truth.

"Two can play at your game, my dear," she said

instead, her face as solid and harsh as ever. She walked out, leaving Nikki to handle the food critic and the crowd alone, the accusations practically hanging in the rafters the same way the red, pink, and white paper hearts did.

Angela, who'd been standing right behind her and had heard everything, stepped up to Nikki and put one arm around her. "Come on, Nik," she whispered, gently turning Nikki away from the retreating back of the woman who had once been Nikki's idol.

Nikki allowed herself to be led back into the kitchen, well aware of the sympathetic look on Beth's face and the worried glint in Jerrod's eye. What she didn't find was the love and support of the one person she needed most.

Paul.

She suddenly knew how deep the hurt between him and his father ran.

Chapter Nineteen

The following morning, Nikki got up before Angela and escaped the apartment. She didn't want to talk about Paul. She didn't want to discuss Holly. She just wanted to be alone.

She walked the early-morning streets of Lakeside, and the day after Valentine's Day, it was a quiet and subdued affair—except for the activity around Delucci's Bakery.

But Nikki couldn't go in there. She hadn't seen Trish and Marty at the pop-up last night; she didn't know what Marty had said to Paul to upset him.

It wasn't Marty, Nikki told herself, turning away from the spot that had always brought a smile to her face. *It was you, Nik. You invited his parents without telling him.*

She sighed and found herself facing Gus's Kitchen, the Café Cupid sign still hanging in the window with all the pink beads and red paper-strip hearts. She still had the key, so she entered the pop-up like she'd be cooking there that night.

But she wouldn't. She didn't want to run the pop-up without Paul, and though he'd said he'd see her today, they didn't have anyone to cook for anyway. Every reservation had been canceled.

It seemed that everything Holly did was done quickly. Four cookbooks in four years. She'd gone from zero to fine dining hero in a matter of weeks. And now she'd spread the rumor all over the city that Nikki's recipes were stolen.

She sighed as she went into the back and got a box. She'd spent so much time schlepping boxes for Holly that her mind seemed permanently stained with the woman.

Nikki pulled down the decorations and placed them almost lovingly in the container. She couldn't believe her dreams of owning a restaurant hadn't even lasted three days. The reality of her situation choked her, but she worked through the debilitating sensation and kept cleaning. After all, Gus would be here soon, and she'd need to turn the keys to the building back over to him.

Her thoughts moved from Holly to the pop-up and, finally, to Paul. Her chest ached, and her head felt hollow. She'd enjoyed working with him, flirting with him at Holly's, cooking with him. She hadn't opened herself up to anyone since Ryan two years ago, and the loss of Paul as a friend and confidant was almost as torturous as not being able to share a kiss with him.

She picked up a small heart made of pink and red strips. She'd stapled one end and then bent the strips into a heart and stapled the other end, turning something straight into something romantic. Tears pressed behind her eyes as she thought about the Valentine's Day dinner Paul had invited her to and then bailed on.

She really should've apologized. Then maybe he wouldn't have run out as soon as the last order was complete. She turned her back on the front windows, fingering the paper heart and wishing hers inside her chest wasn't quite so fragile.

Sighing, she placed the heart on top of the old jukebox she'd loved when she was slinging chili and cornbread in the kitchen, back when Gus was still in business. She drew a deep breath, trying to tame the quivering mess of emotions in her gut, but they wouldn't be calmed by mere oxygen.

Only Paul could do that, and Nikki wasn't sure she'd ever see him again.

The bell on the front door jangled, and she turned to find Gus walking in, his fatherly, kind smile already in place. He reached into his inside jacket pocket and withdrew an envelope.

Nikki managed half of a smile and a near-pathetic wave of her fingers.

"I heard that you had a very successful evening,"

he said, leaning against the jukebox and eyeing the paper heart there.

"It was successful—until Holly Hanson showed up." She dropped her gaze to her fingers, which she couldn't seem to hold still. A smile flashed across her face as she tried to contain the hurt and the tears.

"So you're sure that you don't want the rental for tonight and tomorrow?"

"I would…but last night didn't exactly go as planned." Well, part of it had. They'd sold out. People were taking pictures. Laughing, kissing, enjoying the food.

In that moment, Nikki realized she didn't want a restaurant as a companion. Her real failure last night had been Paul, and he was more important than the pop-up, her recipes, all of it. How could she fix things with him?

She heaved a sigh, her mind a jumbled mess. "And all of our reservations for tonight and tomorrow canceled. So." Gus's usual cheery disposition slipped, mirroring her own sadness. "My whole reputation as a chef has shattered in just one night." The words tasted like poison. They sliced as they settled in her ears. The injustice of what had happened hurt her heart.

He gave a small shake of his head. "You know what I've learned over all these years? That a lie only runs until it's taken over by the truth."

A sliver of hope pushed into her heart and she managed a quick smile. "Thanks, Gus."

He extended the envelope to her, and she took it. "Thanks for the deposit back." She handed over the keys, a small part of her spirit going with them.

"It's not a problem. You know that this place is yours anytime you need it."

She nodded, the strength of her friendship with him still in place. At least he believed in her. A lot of people do, she told herself as she stepped past him to leave. "Bye, Gus."

As she collected her coat, she steeled herself to put Café Cupid in the past. *This doesn't matter. It's a building, a one-night restaurant. What's important is being a good person. Being a good friend.*

Nikki had those kinds of friends, and she wanted them to know she appreciated them standing by her in this mess. Angela had never once asked if the recipes were Nikki's. Beth had only lent her support. Even Jerrod—someone Nikki had only met a month ago—had sacrificed his time and talents to help her.

And Paul…

Paul had become a pillar in her life.

A breath whooshed out of Nikki's mouth. She turned back to Gus, gave him one final wave, and left her dreams behind. But she didn't want to leave the people in her life behind. Now she just had to figure out how to apologize to Paul and fix the rifts she'd caused in their relationship.

Paul barely slept, but when Jerrod texted to see if they were still on for their morning basketball game at the rec center, Paul said yes.

He hadn't been able to think about much besides Nikki. He thought about her as he dressed, as he walked the several blocks to the rec center, as he hung up his coat, and as Jerrod passed him the ball.

Paul tossed it right back, once again reeling over the fact that Nikki had gone into his father's bakery and invited the man to the pop-up. Which might not have been so bad, if she'd—

Jerrod drove past him, and Paul made a late, half-hearted attempt to stop him. Jerrod made the easy layup and let the ball bounce. The sound grated against Paul's nerves.

Everything seemed to be doing that today.

Jerrod collected the ball and tossed it back to Paul. The leather felt foreign in his hand. Nothing seemed to be right in his sphere of existence without Nikki.

You'll see her tonight. He'd walked out last night, but he'd stayed to finish the service. He wouldn't abandon her or their pop-up tonight.

"Not that I mind beating the pants off you," Jerrod said. "But maybe you ought to sit the next one out. Your head's clearly not in the game."

Paul still hadn't bounced the ball. "My head is totally in the game." He threw it back to Jerrod. "Come on."

Jerrod returned it with a hopeful look on his face.

Paul palmed it, but he couldn't bounce it. Had no desire to play. "You know what bothers me most?"

"Ugh. What?" Jerrod's frustration evidently ran as deep as Paul's.

"That she didn't respect me enough to let me know. Tell me he was coming. So I could be prepared, you know?"

"Oh, we're back to that?"

Back to that? That was everything.

"And did I tell you she almost clobbered me with an iron skillet?"

"About three times."

"Just shows you should not get close to someone that you work with." Paul had honestly thought everything he'd told Nikki about maintaining a professional relationship was bunk. But now... She hadn't dumped cayenne pepper in his Bolognese, but his heart felt crushed all the same. Something he'd worked for had been ruined. Something bigger than Bolognese.

Jerrod gave the statement a couple seconds of thought. "Well, Angela and I work together. And we're good."

"So you're taking sides?"

Jerrod held out both hands in placation. "Hey, I'm Switzerland. No side-taking. But I do think it was kind of lousy that you just walked out on her. I mean, your timing just could have been better."

Paul scoffed. "What are you talking about—my timing?"

"Well, for starters, it was Valentine's Day."

Paul knew what day it was. *And you should've known how you leaving would affect Nikki.* His heart had barely been beating since last night. That was why he couldn't sleep, couldn't think, couldn't even bounce a basketball.

"And second, Holly." Jerrod looked at him expectantly, like Paul would have a really great explanation for...Holly?

Paul shook his head, not getting it.

"Did I not tell you?" Jerrod frowned. "Holly...she came by and had some conversation with the big food critic right after you left."

Disbelief—then panic—tore through Paul. He needed to get to Nikki, now.

"Yeah, you forgot to tell me that." Anger at Jerrod replaced his own inadequacies. "How could you forget to tell me that?"

"I just did." He lifted his shoulders in a shrug that said, *Back off, Paul. Not my fault.*

And it certainly wasn't his fault Paul hadn't been there to support Nikki when she'd needed it most. He'd never felt like such a failure, not even when he'd told his dad he didn't want to be a baker.

"I didn't think she was gonna close the place down," Jerrod said. "Since you're partners, I figured you'd know."

Paul inhaled slowly and rubbed his forehead. His brain hurt. "No, I had no idea. I mean, I was planning on seeing her later. For tonight."

"Nope. She canceled it."

"She must have been devastated." Everything that she'd told him about her ex, especially the why behind the breakup, streamed through his mind. And he'd now done the exact same thing.

"She was. She is. But from what Angela tells me, having you mad at her about your dad is equally devastating." Jerrod's underlying message was clear.

Go fix this, man.

Paul slapped the ball and, finally, bounced it one time. The resulting slap of leather on wood reverberated through his head, annoying him further. "I gotta go." He tossed the ball back to Jerrod and returned to the locker room.

He wondered where Nikki was right now. At the café? Sleeping in? He tried calling her, but the line just rang. His frustration boiled, scorching his insides with hot self-loathing.

Shouldering his bag, he went to leave the rec center, determined to trek all over the city to find Nikki. A man shooting hoops with his son caught his attention, and Paul paused.

The boy passed the ball to his dad, who bounce-passed it back. They traded the ball several times, and the boy laughed. The father embraced his son, and Paul's chest squeezed tight. A whole new fear settled over him as he left the rec center, but he didn't see how he could face Nikki without fixing what was really broken first. The kinds of things she'd urged him to fix. Perhaps if he'd done that when she'd suggested it, last night would've been completely different.

Paul's mission morphed. He still needed to find Nikki—but he needed to fix things with his father first.

Chapter twenty

Paul put off going to the bakery until afternoon. He knew it would be less busy then, and he rationalized that he needed to shower first and show up looking nice.

Which was stupid, really. He doubted his parents cared if he was wearing sweats when he came to visit. No, Paul knew he was simply putting off the moment when he'd have to face his father and try to explain.

He tried calling Nikki again but was met with the same result. Ringing line. No answer. Her cute voice telling him to leave a message.

Finally, at about two o'clock, Paul pushed into Delucci's Bakery, the bell announcing his arrival. Sure enough, the place was mostly empty this late in the day, and his father stood at a table, picking up dishes and trash.

"Hey, Dad."

He wiped the table, barely glancing up. "Your mother's in the back."

Wouldn't it be so easy to slip into the back to see her? He shoved his hands into his coat pockets and summoned the courage he needed. "I, ah. I actually came here to see you."

"Look, if it's about the other night—"

"It's not about the other night." Paul shook his head.

"I didn't know...we didn't know—"

"That's not the reason why I'm here—"

"We just wanted to try the—"

"Dad." Paul raised his voice. "I'm trying to tell you something."

"Fine. Talk. I'm listening."

"Don't you think it's time that we got over this silly little feud, so we can just move forward?" Paul gestured from his chest. He really wanted this darkness in his heart to disappear. He hadn't even realized it was there until he'd met Nikki. Her brightness, the way her smile came so quickly, had shown him just how much negativity he was carrying.

"That's what I came here to say."

His father watched him with an intensity Paul felt all the way down into his soul. He gave a little nod for Paul to continue.

"I didn't realize how much it affected me until the other night, when I saw you at the restaurant eating...something that I created." His voice cracked the slightest bit, and he pulled back his emotion. His father had never understood how personal cooking was to Paul.

His dad only looked resigned, and Paul couldn't tell what he was thinking. Dropping his gaze, his dad simply nodded some more, as if he'd heard Paul say all of this before. But Paul hadn't. He'd simply told his father he wanted to go to culinary school and he'd gone.

"Being a chef is what I am good at," Paul said, trying to make his dad understand. "And it's what makes me happy. And as much as I want to please you…I'm not a baker." He'd never said those words so emphatically. He'd never said them at all. "I never will be."

"The truth is, when you decided to go to chef's school, I felt like a failure." His father sounded remorseful, almost on the verge of tears himself.

Surprise caught Paul behind his lungs. He had never realized that his father had felt that way. While he didn't understand why his dad would think he was a failure, he was willing to listen.

"Like I did something wrong, that I let you down somehow." He straightened the teensiest bit. "Listen, I know being a baker isn't as fancy as being a chef, but it's a respectable profession."

"Don't you understand? It's not just your profession." Paul enunciated the words with his hands. How could his father view his baking—this beautiful bakery—as just a job? It was so much more than that, and Paul knew the love he felt for cooking, his father must feel for baking. "You've taken your talent and you've turned it into an art."

He took a deep breath, these new declarations hanging in the air between him and his father. But food could be created, molded, and formed into art. Dough could, too. And it was a passion of his he felt way down deep in his soul. He knew his father felt it, too, or he wouldn't have taken over the bakery from his father and then dedicated his life to it.

"You always wanted to be the best that you could be," Paul said, buoyed by the twinge of a smile that had appeared on his dad's face. "And now you're the best baker this city has ever seen. Just like you, I want to be the best chef that I can be."

"And you are." Those words, spoken with so much authenticity, sank into Paul's soul. He was a good chef, and he knew it. He wanted to be a better person.

"You proved that to me the other night," his dad continued. "Matter of fact, I wanted to tell you then, but when I came to look for you after, you'd already left."

Paul's mom came out from the back, carrying a basket, and Paul glanced at her and then to his dad. A sense of gratitude flowed over him for their support, that they'd come to the pop-up, that his father had enjoyed his food.

But his countenance fell when he thought of why

his dad hadn't been able to find him to tell him in person about the food. "Yeah." He sat at the table his dad had been wiping. "I, uh, I was upset with Nikki for inviting you without telling me."

"She's a good girl, Paul," his mother said. "She had the best intentions."

"I know she is, Ma."

"If you're mad at her for something to do with us, well, then you owe her an apology."

Helplessness filled Paul, almost drowning him. "I know I do, but she won't return my calls." He looked to his father for help.

"She's right, you know." He sat next to Paul and leaned in like he was about to share some life secrets. "Listen, whenever I've done something to upset your mom, I try and think of some way to make her smile."

Paul glanced to his mother, a patient, caring woman who'd stood by her husband for decades. He couldn't help smiling at her. Wild questions bounced around his mind. What would it take to make Nikki smile again? Could he be the one to cause it?

"A gesture," his dad said. "A genuine gesture from the heart goes a long way."

"You're right. You're absolutely right." He put his hand on his dad's arm, the emotion and forgiveness flowing between them thick—so thick it made his throat constrict. "Okay. Thanks, Dad."

Paul got up and headed for the door, an idea swirling through different stages in his brain. How could he show Nikki he was sorry about breaking their Valentine's Day dinner date and not being there to support her when Holly had shown up?

Nikki wanted a restaurant more than anything else. How could he make that a reality for her?

The gesture had dozens of moving pieces, but he could put one in place—a location. He called Gus, who agreed to meet him at the diner any time Paul wanted.

"Let me make a few more calls," Paul said. "And I'll let you know."

With five years of experience in the restaurant industry, he had no qualms about his ability to get a new place going. But what he really needed to do was repair the damage Holly had done to Nikki's reputation as a cook.

It was a David versus Goliath feat. Nikki had said there had been surveillance footage on Holly's computer. He'd need that video, the contact info for the food critic who'd come to Café Cupid, and someone who had more influence than he did. Some money would be excellent, too.

Not only all of that, but someone with knowledge of Holly Hanson—the woman or the restaurant— would be helpful, as well.

Henry. Holly's investor popped into his head almost like it wasn't his own thought. But Henry was the perfect person to help Paul get a new restaurant off the ground. He had the media contacts. He had the money. And most importantly, he had the ability to discredit Holly.

Henry could probably help get the security footage as well. If Paul could convince him just to take a look at the surveillance videos, he might be able to get the proof he needed. And if Henry knew Holly had stolen the recipes, he'd do something about it.

The idea morphed and twisted, turned and formed. He extracted his phone from his pocket and made the phone call, praying that Henry would pick up a call from him, though he didn't work for Holly anymore.

Thankfully, he did, and Paul's plan solidified even more.

"When can you meet?" Henry asked.

"Anytime," Paul said. "Now." He pressed his eyes closed. "I'd like to meet at the diner where Nikki and I had our pop-up. Can you come over to Gus's Kitchen?"

"Sure," Henry said. "Be there in a few minutes."

Paul called Gus, who said he could meet Paul there with a key, leaving Paul only the time it took for him to walk from the bakery to Café Cupid to get his thoughts together.

When he arrived, Gus waved, settling Paul's thoughts, and he entered the place where he'd thought he'd be cooking that night. Hopefully, if all went according to his plan, he'd have a lot more nights spent in this kitchen.

Henry turned when Paul entered, the chime alerting him to the arrival.

"Henry, thanks for coming to meet me." He extended his hand for Henry to shake as Gus slid over in the booth to make room for Paul.

"No problem at all."

Paul sat across from Henry, hoping he could crack the man's tough exterior. He'd never actually seen Henry smile.

"So. What did you want to talk to me about?"

"I have some interesting news," Paul said. "That you might find hard to believe."

"I'm all ears."

Paul drew a deep breath and glanced at Gus, who gave him an encouraging nod. "Holly's recipes aren't hers," Paul said. "They really are Nikki Turner's…"

Nikki needed another job, but she was wary of putting herself out there in the restaurant industry. She reasoned that she had a few days to spare before things got really desperate, so she spent them at the community center, helping those who were already worse off than her.

With Holly Hanson's still closed for the renovations, Angela had taken to joining her. Nikki was really grateful for her friend's support, for brewing the coffee in the morning, and for making sure Nikki had time to express how she felt about everything.

She needed to call her dad, who had been such a

big help with getting the pop-up restaurant off the ground. He'd called once and left a message, wanting to know how things had gone during the three-day pop-up.

Nikki didn't have the heart to call him back and tell him she'd only had one day in her restaurant. And she didn't want her parents to know that she'd been accused of stealing recipes. She needed to include her parents in her life—her real life, not just the good things—but her humiliation still burned strongly in the back of her mouth.

I'll call them after lunch.

She wiped tables after the busy shift, and Nikki turned to find Angela staring at a newspaper. As she approached, Ang quickly folded it in half and tucked it under her arm.

"Why are you hiding that newspaper?"

She turned and faced Nikki, her eyebrows lifting high. "Because I'm your best friend and I'm trying to protect you."

"From what?" Nikki's gaze fell to the newspaper, still mostly out of sight. Her anxiety fired, sending little shockwaves through her. She thought she'd gotten used to the idea of everyone thinking she was a thief and a fraud, but apparently not.

How does one get used to that, anyway?

Angela stared her down for several seconds before relenting. "There's a review of Café Cupid."

"Well, what does it say?" She didn't mean to snap,

but her anger seemed so close to the surface since Valentine's Day.

"Nothing. Nikki," Angela said in a placating, almost pleading tone. "You don't want to read this."

"Yes, I do." She snatched the newspaper from Angela and flipped it open. She found the article easily with the giant, all-capped title of HOLLY'S RECIPES STOLEN right there at the top.

Her heart fell to her shoes and rebounded back to her chest, an uncomfortable feeling that left all of her internal organs out of whack.

"Nikki Turner's recipes are, in fact, those of her former employer, Holly Hanson," she read. "So it's no surprise that this menu was spectacular." She gave a fake giggle and glanced at Angela, who shifted uncomfortably.

"Holly Hanson's reopens for business this week, and I encourage all food lovers to drop by, as you won't be disappointed. Your taste buds will thank you." She scanned the other print like there would be something redeeming for her there. Of course, there wasn't. She flopped the paper down onto the table, that keen sense of disbelief and horror winding through her again.

It coiled around her heart and squeezed, threaded itself through her lungs and gripped tightly. So tight she couldn't breathe. She pushed out a breath, trying to figure out what to do. Where to go from here. How to move on.

It's so unfair that Holly—

Nikki's thoughts paused.

Holly.

She reached for her apron and fumbled with the ties along her waist. "You know what? I gotta go. I just—I gotta go." She threw down her apron and marched away.

"Wait. Where are you going?" Angela called after her.

Nikki didn't slow, didn't turn back. She simply grabbed her coat and said, "To tackle my inspiration."

Chapter twenty-One

With only one more day until the grand reopening, Holly was working long hours. Her new assistant wasn't nearly as competent as Nikki, and Holly had to correct her on multiple items. She'd gone so far as to make the woman check with her on everything before it was actually done.

Jayda approached, and Holly's patience went flying out the window. Jayda held up the fifth mock-up of the new menu, and Holly examined it.

"Hmm, you should feature the chicken closer to the top. And, um, be sure to mention the ice cream cones. People find those fascinating."

Jayda nodded in tight jabs, the fear on her face fading. "Sure thing."

Holly turned her back on her, a clear dismissal, and returned to the checklist she needed to go through with the painters before she paid them.

"Holly?"

She glanced up to find Nikki Turner standing in her restaurant. Holly froze. Did she somehow have proof that the recipes were hers? Holly had deleted the surveillance footage, even going so far as to tape over the hard copies so no one would ever see Nikki cooking waffle fried chicken in the middle of the night in Holly Hanson's kitchen.

"There's something I have to say to you. Something I need to say." Nikki took a couple steps closer.

Holly put on her I'm-in-control face. "Why don't you talk to my lawyer?"

"No, that won't be necessary. You've been such an inspiration to me." A smile actually formed on the younger woman's face, and a truckload of guilt dumped through Holly.

"As a young, aspiring chef, I looked up to you. To me, Holly Hanson was a chef who had integrity, and fierceness, and originality."

Holly squinted at Nikki but couldn't find an ounce of guile in her. She longed for the days when she'd had her integrity, her fierceness, and her originality. But the restaurant business and the publishing business, not to mention the fame, had chewed her up and spit her out an unrecognizable person, even to herself.

"You were, in every sense of the word, my idol."

Out of the corner of her eye, Holly caught movement. She didn't look away from Nikki, who seemed near tears, but she made out the form of Henry.

"But now I know the truth. That to achieve the

success that you've had, a chef has to be underhanded and dishonest."

Holly had never seen Nikki anything but bubbly and pleasant, even after going through dozens of heavy boxes in a single day. But this version of Nikki was upset, and rightfully so. Still, Holly couldn't bring herself to say anything. She knew her lawyer wouldn't like it if she did.

And in that moment, she realized exactly what kind of person she was—and it wasn't anyone's idol.

"And that is a person I never want to become," Nikki said, lifting her chin. "So, you can steal my recipes. And you can destroy my reputation. But there is one thing that you will never take, and that is my spirit. You might think you've won, but I just need you to know that you didn't beat me." Nikki didn't wait for Holly to respond. She simply turned and left the restaurant, her head held high.

Holly actually envied her, as she couldn't hold her head very high. Not very high at all. She did manage to glance in Henry's direction, and from the look on his face, she knew Nikki's conversation wasn't the last hard one she'd be having that evening.

To her surprise, he simply shook his head, a look of pure disgust on his face, and followed Nikki out.

Out.

Gone.

Holly couldn't reopen without paying the painters. And she couldn't pay the painters without

Henry's investment in her restaurant. As she watched him retreat, she knew everything she'd worked for, everything she'd lied about, the recipes she'd stolen, was ending.

Over.

Gone.

Nikki felt freer than she had since Valentine's Day. Living under the weight of what people thought about her had been suffocating, almost completely debilitating. But she'd spoken true. Holly had not beaten her.

She walked down the street, her step sure and her spirit lighter than it had been in a while. She'd get another job, find something worthwhile to fill her life with, make her way in this city.

Her phone rang, interrupting her introspection. She pulled the device out of her pocket and saw Paul's name on the screen.

He'd called several times over the past few days, and she'd never answered. She wasn't sure what to say to him, how to explain in a way he would understand. The thing was, she'd lost more than him. She'd lost her friendship with his parents, too, and she sighed as she decided to answer the call.

After all, it was silly to avoid such delicious lattes and biscotti.

"Hello?" she said.

"Listen, I know you don't want to talk to me, but could you come and meet me at Gus's Kitchen?" He spoke in rapid, machine-gun-fire words. He finally breathed. "I have something I want to show you."

Why not? She couldn't think of a good reason, other than her heart was already in tatters. "Yeah. I'll come meet you."

"Bye." He hung up before she could say anything. She wasn't sure what he could possibly want to show her at Gus's. Nikki had cleaned up all the decorations and given back the keys. Maybe he wanted his deposit back. She stopped by her apartment on the way to collect the envelope. She didn't want there to be anything between them, especially money.

He'd sounded pleasant enough, so perhaps he wasn't upset with her. But she couldn't fathom why she needed to go to Gus's. Anticipation and hope battled inside her nervous system, and she kept pushing back the optimism.

Be sure to apologize, she told herself. See what he wants, and then apologize. By the time she rounded the corner, almost an hour had passed. Paul stood with his back to her, looking all tall and delicious under the orange street lamp.

Her heart thudded painfully at the simple sight of him, and she hoped she could make it through this conversation without revealing too much or breaking down. "Hey."

He spun toward her, a guarded look in his eye. She didn't know what he wanted or how he felt, and the need to protect herself reared. "Uh, listen, before I forget, here's your security deposit back."

He stared at the envelope like it was covered in manure. He finally put his fingers on it, and she let go, refolding her arms to try to keep her emotion contained.

Paul looked at her, and she glanced away so she wouldn't fall into his crystal blue eyes. "So why did you want to meet me here?"

He took a deep breath and released it. "Look, I know I was wrong for blaming you. You were just trying to do the right thing. And I know how hurtful it was that I left you."

She watched him but couldn't find any signs of a fib. Paul had never been disingenuous with her. He'd been nothing but kind, funny, and supportive—at least until Valentine's Day night.

"But even more so for not sticking around when you and Holly had your falling out. The fact is, you deserve so much better."

His words caused warmth to stream through her, along with a healthy dose of confusion. "I'm not really following."

"What I'm trying to say is that I'm really not that type of person. The type of person that doesn't stick around. Who doesn't support the people he…cares about."

Nikki's pulse skidded against her ribcage. She could hear his affection for her in his words. See it right there in his eyes. She allowed a smile to grace her face, the possibility of her and Paul too much to contain behind straight lips.

"Nikki, that night was perfect. The crowd. The food. The space. You and I. We were...perfect. And then when I saw my dad, it threw me, and I took it out on you."

"Paul, I'm so sorry." Finally, the apology she'd needed to say for days had been vocalized.

"Don't be. I'm thankful, because without you, I never would have made up with him."

"You made up?" Hope, that blessed hope she'd been searching for the last few days, finally returned.

"Yeah."

"That's awesome." Nikki wondered if he was looking to complete additional make-ups, and she realized that she really wanted him to be. "But, um, still doesn't really answer what we're doing here."

"We're here because..." He reached into his pocket and pulled out a set of jingle-jangly keys. "I have the keys."

She looked at them and then at him, still trying to piece it all together. He didn't offer any further explanation—at least not verbally. He turned and stepped toward the door to Gus's, which he unlocked, and then ushered her inside.

Nikki went, because she wanted to be with Paul.

Needed to drink in the intoxicating scent of his cologne and hope for a future together with him.

Once inside, he took off his coat like he was planning to stay awhile. But it was already late, and the diner certainly wasn't set up to open any time soon.

She giggled, partly because of nerves and partly because it felt so good to be with him as he grinned and seemed so at ease. "What's going on?"

He hung up his coat and clapped his hands together. "Welcome to Café Cupid Two-point-oh."

Nikki put her coat on the rack next to his. "What? I'm confused. We're doing another pop-up restaurant?"

"No, we aren't. We're opening up a new, permanent restaurant." He couldn't seem to stop smiling, and he never once looked away from her.

"Wait, how can we afford this? I mean, it takes months for a restaurant to recover. And what about that review? Everyone thinks I'm a fraud."

"We just happen to have a very influential new investor."

Her mind spun, and she could barely keep up with the conversation, let alone what it all meant. "Wait, an influential investor?"

"Henry. He's no longer with Holly. He's with us now. He called that critic, who's going to be retracting their story, and they're going to be writing a new, splashy article on you. Your recipes. And your new space."

Her smile felt huge. While she'd been cooking

lunch and dinner at the community center and trying to figure out how to apologize, Paul had been doing something amazing. Something grand.

"I don't know what to say." She looked at him, letting out all the things she'd been holding back—especially the desire to move past professional and into personal with Paul.

His expression softened, too, almost like he knew this was more than a business transaction to her. Of course he did. She could see the love right there in his eyes. She hoped hers were saying it back.

"Say yes." He extended his hand toward her, the same way he had on Valentine's Day night when he'd asked her to dance. She remembered the warmth and comfort of his arms, of being so close to him, both in body and spirit.

She took his hand, though there was no music. He grinned in that sexy, sly way he had and drew her into his arms—right where she belonged.

He moved them in a slow circle, the movement intimate and intoxicating, as he gazed down at her. "Nikki Turner, will you be my Valentine?"

"Valentine's Day passed."

"Consider it a standing reservation for next year." He swayed, taking her with him, and lifted his hand from hers to cup her face as he leaned down to kiss her. She wrapped her fingers around the back of his neck, every nerve firing with white-hot energy as his lips touched hers for the first time.

Nikki knew this kiss was better than any she could've received on Valentine's Day. Because this was a kiss with a man who knew her, understood her, and wanted to love and support her every day of the year.

Epilogue

"The new tables are here," Paul said as soon as he hung up.

Nikki turned from her prep station at the back of the kitchen. "Oh yeah?"

"I'm going to go get them." He swept toward her and took her in his arms. "Want to come?"

"I have to work on the pork loins," she said, giggling as he traced his lips along her neck. "You should be working on the pork loins."

She was right; he should be working on his signature Valentine's Day dish. But the tables were here, and he'd been waiting for them for three months. They were the final piece he and Nikki needed to transform the space they'd built together into what they really wanted it to be.

He put his hands around her waist, and she relaxed into his chest. "It's just pork loin," he said.

"You're wrong about that, mister. It's the whole reason we're booked out for the next week."

"The tables complete the space." He released her and turned back to where they'd started their pop-up restaurant almost one year ago. She'd loved the diner atmosphere, but her recipes were too high-end to match the décor.

"It doesn't have to be stuffy to represent fine food," she'd argued, mentioning how crayons could create art.

Paul got it. He did. It was the fact that the food was cooked with a dash of love that made her recipes special. It was the chemistry they shared in the kitchen, the creativity she sparked in him, and the playful way she combined flavors.

It definitely wasn't diner food, and they shouldn't be serving it in a diner, as he'd said over and over.

When he'd mentioned the word "bistro," he'd captured Nikki's attention. They'd poured over pictures of trendy bistros with all-brick feature walls and sophisticated furniture. Down-home bistros with blue-and-white checkered tablecloths and fresh flowers on the table. Classic bistros with black-and-white motifs and splatter art on the walls.

None of them had felt quite right to Paul and Nikki. She wanted bright and colorful, which mirrored who she was inside and out. He wanted classic and clean, which identified his style of cooking.

They'd met in the middle with a design that included some rustic wood on the wall Paul had installed himself, and white arches in the ceilings to add the charming, homey, open feel Nikki wanted.

Paul had pulled out the booths, and they'd been renting tables and chairs from a restaurant supply store for a few months.

But their new permanent tables were here. A smile broke onto his face and she swatted his arm. "Go get your tables."

He practically skipped out of the restaurant. Her pink and gray tablecloths would look fantastic with the black iron tables and the butterscotch-colored chairs. She just didn't know it yet.

He'd learned that Nikki could envision food with ease, but everything else took a bit more work. So he'd worked at it. Created menus with her. Tweaked recipes. He'd even gone so far as to draw up sketches with the ideas he had.

And tonight, the first night they were serving their Valentine's Day menu, everything would finally come together.

His phone rang as he pulled into the restaurant supply company. They'd promised they could send a crew to take down the rental tables and chairs and put up the new, permanent furniture, and he hoped they weren't backing out now.

But it wasn't their number.

"Hello?" he answered.

"Paul Delucci?"

"This is him."

"It's Bryan Roosevelt at Double R Jewelers. I'm just calling to let you know the ring you sent out for resizing and cleaning has come back."

Paul's heart stuttered-stepped. The ring he'd designed for Nikki.

"You can come pick it up anytime," Bryan continued.

"Thanks," Paul said, his voice a bit numb, echoing how he felt inside. He and Nikki had been together for a year, and he wanted to take their relationship to the next level. And the next level included diamonds and I do's.

At least, he hoped it did.

He faced the entrance, beyond which sat his table and chairs, as well as the completion of their bistro. After this, he could focus on the completion of their future.

So he exhaled, pushed the diamond ring to the back of his mind, and entered the store. A vast array of chairs, linens, and silverware met his eyes.

"Paul," someone called.

He turned to find his rep striding toward him. "Mike, hey." The two men shook hands, and Mike turned down one of the aisles in the vast warehouse. "Your tables are back here. I've got my crew ready to load them as soon as you inspect them and sign off."

Giddiness paraded through him, and he couldn't believe he was so excited about tables and chairs.

"Did your father like them?" Mike asked.

"Yeah," Paul said. "He said he might go with black iron next time he remodels the bakery."

"Oh, his tables and chairs are perfect for what he does there." Mike glanced over his shoulder. "He doesn't need the sophistication of black iron. His wood is comfortable and casual, just what people want to eat Italian pastries."

"I'll tell him you said that." Paul chuckled. "Mom always wants to change things up, but Dad's more resistant."

"Here we are." Mike gestured to the nineteen tables that had already been assembled. The harsh overhead lights shone on the black legs and the bright, bleached wood tops.

Paul ran his hand along the closest table, his dreams and vision for D&T's finally coming together. A smile stretched across his face. "These look great. Let's get it all over to the bistro."

Mike plucked a radio off his hip and spoke into it. Only a minute later, several men joined Paul and Mike, and they started loading up the tables and chairs.

"I'll meet you back over there," Paul said, wondering if he had time to stop by the jewelry store. His heart raced in anticipation of seeing the restaurant all put together the way he and Nikki had envisioned.

But he also wanted to put that ring on her finger as soon as possible.

The plan was Valentine's Day, he told himself as

he made his way past all the rental supplies and back to his car.

And Valentine's Day was still six days away.

So Paul reset his focus once again and went back to the restaurant downtown. "I'm going to pull the tablecloths off," he said. "You should see these tables, Nik. They're so great. And the chairs are really going to add that pop of color you want."

He moved their centerpieces onto the serving bar as she said, "We open for lunch in an hour."

"They're on their way." He flashed her a grin and continued working.

"I'll help." She left her station in the kitchen and, in no time, they had all the rental equipment ready to be whisked away.

Paul reached for Nikki's hand as the supply store truck pulled in front of the bistro. "D&T's," he said, squeezing.

She'd come up with the name for their restaurant, taking the first letter from each of their last names. It was trendy, and Paul had liked it instantly. They'd needed something more permanent than Café Cupid and not as pretentious as naming it after one of them. Besides, they were a team.

The chime on the door went off, giving the place a classic diner atmosphere, and men worked to remove plain white tables and chairs, which had sufficed but hadn't added any real flavor to the dining experience.

As the new furniture came in, Paul thought his

heart would burst from his chest. He hadn't felt this level of happiness, ever. A beautiful woman he loved at his side, his own restaurant coming to life right in front of him.

He met Nikki's eye and they laughed together before he leaned down and kissed her squarely on the mouth. "I love you," he whispered before releasing her and reaching for a pink and gray tablecloth.

Nikki basked in Paul's enthusiasm. He'd been so optimistic about their restaurant, and their hard work had paid off. He'd put in long hours in the kitchen, long hours on the renovation of the space, and long hours making sure she knew he was there to support her.

She watched him lay the tablecloth over the table lovingly, and her heart warmed. The black iron was beautiful, and it added a nice contrast to the light walls and bright arches. He'd been right—as usual.

Picking up a pile of cloth, she got to work resetting the tables, too. Her vintage cups and pitchers held fresh flowers, and she placed them in the middle as centerpieces next to salt and pepper shakers, sugar substitute packets, and a house-made barbeque sauce Paul had perfected last fall.

With the crew of men, plus Paul and Nikki, the bistro came together in only a few minutes. It felt like someone could enjoy great food and great friends in a great atmosphere.

It was everything she'd ever wanted. Her smile couldn't have gotten any bigger or brighter as she surveyed the bistro. "It's gorgeous," she whispered as Paul stepped into the kitchen.

He returned a few moments later wearing his chef's jacket and carrying an apron. "It's great, right? Do you like it?"

She turned toward him. "I love it." She launched herself into his arms and held on tightly as he chuckled and spun her around. He set her on her feet and gazed down on her with that powerful, intimate way he had. "I love you," she said, stretching up to kiss him.

Lunch service went off without a hitch, and in the dead time between lunch and dinner, they served a few sandwiches and plates of pasta. Dinner prep and cleaning happened, and Nikki loved the dance they shared in the kitchen. She appreciated her waitstaff, her hostess, and everyone else who labored in the back of the house with dishes.

She'd been working on some little gifts for everyone for their one-year anniversary. She'd counted the partnership starting on the first night their pop-up had opened last year, so that anniversary was just a few short days away.

Nikki had gone through trinkets and water bottles, cards and gift certificates. She'd finally settled on gifting what she was best at—food. She rather liked the idea of a fancy invitation to an employees-only event at D&T's, which she would be cooking and serving to everyone.

Paul knew nothing about it, and she wanted to keep it that way. So she kept the little secret under her tongue, smiling every time she thought about it.

"Hey, I have to run out for a minute," Paul said, drawing her attention from her covert anniversary plans.

"You do?" She looked at him, but he didn't meet her eye. "Where are you going?"

"I just, uh, have to go pick something up." He gave her one of his classic, crinkly-eyed smiles and pressed his lips to her forehead. "I'll be gone thirty minutes, tops." He practically ran out of the restaurant, and Nikki watched him with narrowed eyes.

That man was up to something, she just knew it.

Valentine's Day arrived, and Nikki rose early to get to the bistro before anyone else. She laid out the immaculate invitation cards she'd been working on for a solid week and stood behind the counter as each member of D&T's entered.

Ang got there first, her eyebrows lifting at the display. "You didn't want to come in together this morning?"

Nikki giggled and pointed to the cards. "Find yours."

Angela scanned them. "What is this?" She picked

up the one with her name on it. "D&T's one-year anniversary," she read. "You're invited to a special meal designed and cooked by Nikki. February fifteenth, six o'clock." Angela looked at her. "You're cooking for the staff?"

She lifted one shoulder into a shrug, hoping this idea wasn't too lame. "It's just that you guys do so much for me and Paul, and we can't run the restaurant without everyone. I wanted to say thanks." She pressed her lips together, her excitement almost getting the best of her. "Paul cooks for everyone all the time, but I didn't even tell him. So."

"Of course I'll be here." Angela hugged her and went to hang her coat in the back.

"What is all this?"

Nikki spun to find Paul surveying the invitations on the counter. He met her eye, questions in his.

"You cook for everyone every Sunday," she said, referencing the tradition he'd brought with him from Holly Hanson's. "I wanted to do something special for our one-year anniversary."

He picked up the navy invitation and ran his finger along the edge of it. "What are you serving?"

"Uh-uh." She pushed him in the chest, nudging him back a foot or two. "Not telling. It's a surprise."

"Does it have anything to do with the load of filet mignon that was just delivered?" He hooked his thumb toward the back, that crinkly smile she'd fallen in love with appearing on his face.

Nikki's face fell, her playfulness gone. "It's here?" She strained onto her toes to see behind him and into the kitchen.

"The supplier got here at the same time I did. I was surprised to see the beef, as it's not on our Valentine's Day menu."

"It's my menu."

He tapped her on the nose. "I can see that now."

"You're impossible to surprise. You know that, don't you?" She wished she had a wooden spoon to wag at him, the same way she'd flirted with him in his own kitchen over a year ago.

He laughed and wrapped her in a tight embrace. "I feel like I never have a moment alone with you," he said, his voice dropping to a whisper by the end of his sentence. "Remember how I asked you to be my Valentine last year?"

How could she forget? "Yeah." She laid her cheek against his chest, a sense of contentment cascading through her.

"How about a private dinner tonight, just the two of us? After everyone else goes home."

"Sounds wonderful," she murmured.

By the time they finished serving four rounds of reservations, Nikki's exhaustion lived in every cell in her body.

"Do you want the pork loin?" he asked. Paul never

seemed to run out of energy, something Nikki envied about him.

She yawned. "Yeah."

"You go sit," he said. "I'll bring it out when it's ready."

She didn't argue with him, though she loved being in the kitchen with him. She wandered into the alley where they'd shared their first dance, but there were no tea lights tonight, no paper lanterns. It was just an alley.

So she went back into the restaurant and chose her favorite table, the one closest to the windows where all the city lights shone in. A long sigh escaped her lips as she sat, and she rubbed the back of her neck, which was often sore from her long days and nights bent over a saucepan and then a plate as she put every little piece in place.

"All the way out there," Paul said as he exited the kitchen and found her across the bistro. "I see how you are."

"Tired is how I am." Nikki smiled at him gratefully as he set a couple of wine glasses on the table and then the beautiful pork loin for two they'd been serving all night.

"Red wine?" he asked.

"Mm." She nodded, her mouth watering from the delicious scent of roasted meat and the tantalizing crispness of the potatoes.

He returned a few moments later with the wine

and poured them each a glass. She reached for hers, but he didn't even sit down.

She glanced up at him. "Aren't you—?"

"Nikki, I need to talk to you about something."

She set the wine glass down, a tremor shooting through her. "All right."

He dropped to one knee beside her, sending her heart toward the stars.

"Nikki, this has been the best year of my life." His eyes streamed emotion toward her, and her breath stuck in her throat.

"You and I are so good together, and I want to be with you for always." He brought a black ring box out from behind his back. The lid made a creaking sound as he opened it to reveal a gorgeous diamond set in a thick rose gold band.

Nikki's eyes widened, and she looked from the engagement ring to Paul, who wore a look of pure hope on his face. Shock shot down to her toes. He was so good at surprises. So good at picking out and presenting gifts. She adored that about him.

"Will you marry me?" he asked, his voice husky.

Nikki's lifelong dream had been to open her own restaurant, but that had already happened. And it was wonderful and something she enjoyed every day.

But with Paul, she'd come to see that a restaurant—even a trendy bistro—wasn't what made her life complete.

He made her life complete—his presence by her side, his unselfishness, his love for her.

And she loved him.

"Yeah, I mean, yes, of course I will." She sprang to her feet and embraced him. Her legs trembled, but he held her upright in his strong arms, a laugh starting in his chest. She giggled, too, twining her higher-pitched voice to his.

"Let me put the ring on," he said, pulling back a little bit. He extracted the jewelry from the box. "I had it sent out for sizing, so it should fit." His fingers on hers were warm, solid, as he slid the ring on. "It's beautiful." He gazed at her finger, and Nikki had a hard time looking away, too.

"You're beautiful. I love you, Nikki Turner."

"I love you, Paul." She grinned and squealed as he lifted her off her feet. He kissed her, and she kissed him back, the moment turning heated and serious.

He grinned, breaking their connection, and Nikki gazed up at him, full of love and adoration for such a wonderful man. Sure, she'd been through a lot since she'd met Paul, but the darkness only allowed the brighter parts of her life to come into fuller realization. She could experience this absolute joy with Paul because she'd been in the depths of sorrow.

And there was no one else she'd rather experience every high and every low with. If they could add a dash of love to whatever they did, they'd be just fine.

THE END

Beef Chili with Cinnamon

A Hallmark Original Recipe

At the beginning of *A Dash of Love*, Nikki's delicious chili at the diner has a secret ingredient: cinnamon candies. These really do add the perfect touch of spice and sweetness to a recipe you'll turn to again and again.

> **Yield:** 8 servings
> **Prep Time:** 30 minutes
> **Cook Time:** 3 hours
> **Total Time:** 3½ hours

INGREDIENTS

- 3 lb. beef chuck roast
- ½ teaspoon kosher salt
- ½ teaspoon black pepper
- ¼ cup extra virgin olive oil, divided
- 1 large onion, diced
- 1 red bell pepper, diced
- 4 garlic cloves, minced
- 2 tbsp. chili powder
- 1½ tbsp. ground cumin
- 1 teaspoon dried oregano
- 2 (10-oz.) cans diced tomatoes & green chilies
- 1 (14½-oz.) can diced tomatoes
- 1 (12-oz.) bottle dark beer (such as stout)
- 1 (16-oz.) can chili beans
- 1 (16-oz.) can kidney beans, drained
- 2 tbsp. cinnamon flavored candies
- as needed, sour cream
- as needed, fresh diced avocado
- as needed, green onions, chopped
- as needed, tortilla chips
- as needed, fresh cilantro sprigs

DIRECTIONS

1. Preheat oven to 325°F.
2. Slice chuck roast into bite-size cubes, trimming excess fat as needed; season with salt and pepper.
3. Heat 2 tablespoons olive oil in a large heavy

pot or Dutch oven. Add beef and brown over medium-high heat, stirring frequently, until all moisture has evaporated and beef is browned. Remove from pot and set aside.

4. Add 2 tablespoons olive oil to pot; add onion and saute over medium-low heat for 5 minutes, stirring frequently. Add bell pepper and garlic; saute an additional 5 minutes.

5. Add browned beef back to pot; add spices and stir to blend. Add beer and diced tomatoes; stir to blend.

6. Cover and transfer pot to oven; oven-bake for 2½ hours.

7. Remove from oven; add beans and cinnamon candies. Return to oven and bake an additional 15 minutes. Taste and adjust seasoning, if needed.

8. Serve chili topped with sour cream, avocado, green onions, tortilla chips and cilantro, if desired.

Thanks so much for reading *A Dash of Love*. We hope you enjoyed it!

For information about our new releases and exclusive offers, sign up for our free newsletter at hallmarkchannel.com/hallmark-publishing-newsletter

You can also connect with us here:

Facebook.com/HallmarkPublishing

Twitter.com/HallmarkPublish

CPSIA information can be obtained
at www.ICGtesting.com
Printed in the USA
LVHW11s1235201018
594259LV00001B/1/P